LOVED BY THE HIGHLAND WOLF

STEPHANIE MARKS

RED DAGGER

FOREWORD

A NOTE TO MY READERS

I hope that you enjoy this book. If you are interested in finding out about my latest releases, be sure to visit my website to sign up for my newsletter.

StephanieMarks.com

~ Stephanie

EXCERPT

He stood too close to me, the toes of his boots almost touching those of my slippers. He raised his hands and rested them on the shelf behind me, effectively caging me in.

That was what came of thinking of him like a friend instead of my captor. I should never have joked with him so freely. I couldn't breathe with him so close.

"Are ye afraid of me, lass?"

I swallowed and shook my head. "No, it's just a bit... unnerving. You are nothing like what I was expecting. I thought you would be... wild... and cruel."

"And now?" His deep voice was low, barely above a whisper. I looked up into his vivid green eyes and resisted the urge to touch him.

"Now I just think you're wild. But how could you not be, being what you are?"

"Aye, lass, I'm wild."

"And dangerous," I whispered.

"Why do ye say that?" he asked, leaning closer.

"Because when you're near me like this, I cannot think straight. I forget who I am and how I came to be here. I forget my loneliness. I forget everything but how badly..." I shook my head, trying to clear it of the fog. "How badly I want you to touch me."

He lifted a hand to cup my cheek, then trailed his fingers down and around the back of my neck.

"If anyone here is dangerous, lass, it's you..."

CHAPTER 1

I stood frozen in fear, struggling to breathe as the crisp winter air attacked my lungs like shards of jagged glass. Bright amber eyes stared back into mine, burning straight into the core of me, and surrounding those eyes was... nothing. There was nothing but a dark screaming void, reaching out to me. Ready to drag me down into the darkness.

I tore my gaze away, desperate to be free, and the darkness was replaced by blinding white snow. The forest was eerily quiet. Not a single animal or rustling of trees was to be heard. I looked down to see my mother lying in the snow, her eyes wide and her mouth open in a scream. Her throat had been torn out, and her blood was splashed across the virgin canvas of the forest floor.

A snap came from behind me. A branch breaking. My whole body tensed as I turned slowly toward the sound. It had come back for me.

The giant wolf lunged at my face, huge jaws open wide, and I let out a bloodcurdling scream...

I sat up in bed in a flurry of blankets and pillows, looking wildly around the chamber for the great savage beast I knew to be lurking in the corners of my room. My heart beat like a war drum on the eve of battle and I clutched at my sweat-drenched shift, slowly coming to the realization that it was just a dream. It had only been a dream.

I hadn't had the nightmare in years, not since I was a child. But it had come to me three times now over the last fortnight, and each dream was more vivid than the one before.

I lay back in bed and pulled the covers up to my chin. The air was chill in the castle and I had no fire to warm me. I inhaled deeply through my nose and out through my mouth in an effort to calm myself, but the beat of my heart refused to slow. The burning amber eyes continued to float in front of my face in the darkness as if seared into my vision, and closing my eyes only served to make them appear more vivid instead of blocking them out.

Sighing in defeat I threw back the blankets and got out of bed. I walked across the cold stone floor to my window and looked up into the sky. The partial moon shone down over the Gordon lands, illuminating the hills behind the keep, and I rubbed my arms against the chill of the highland air.

I winced as my stomach rumbled in hunger. I had not eaten much at supper and was paying for it now, just as my father had said I would. It had been foolish of me to not think to bring something back with me to eat in case the mood struck, but there was naught for me to do about it now. I would just have to sneak down to the kitchens in search of something.

As I made my way through the halls in the dark I heard the low murmuring of voices coming from one of the rooms. The closer I got the more I could make out the heated voice of my uncle, and then my father's.

Curious as to what they were arguing about downstairs in the middle of the night, I crouched low outside the closed door to listen.

"We have no other choice, Cameron. It's the only way," my uncle insisted.

"No, Dougal, I'll nay hear any more about it. We must come up with another way. I'd rather tear out my own heart and feed it to the savage MacGregor myself before I'd go along with your plan. Have you gone completely mad, man?"

I gasped at my father's words. They were fighting over the dreaded highland chief, Alastair MacGregor. The man, if in fact he was a man and not a beast from the deepest pits of hell as the rumors claimed, was a fierce warrior. It was said that he rode into battle with a pack of giant wolves at his side that tore his enemies to pieces with their monstrous jaws.

The image from my dream came back to me and I shivered, inching closer to the door in order to hear more clearly.

"Ye cannot avoid this forever, Cameron, and ye know it. The rider came this very night. You've looked upon the warning with your own eyes. The MacGregor is moving this way and will be upon us within the week. Maybe you're right and it's just a matter of a simple reiving he's after. Maybe he'll not even come all this way. But ye know as well as I that he cannot be trusted to think like a normal man. We cannot just ignore this and hope he goes around us. And even if he leaves us be this time, ye know it won't last forever. Sooner or later it will be our turn. He'll slaughter our men and rape our women, then take the children for slaves. Are ye willing to let your people meet that fate all because you're feeling sentimental? And you've got the gall to stand there and call yourself our chief?"

I jumped at the sound of a fist coming down hard on wood. My father was a kind and understanding man, but my uncle ran the risk of seeing his seldom-shown temper by insulting him that way.

"Dinna push me on this, Dougal. I'll not be changing my mind on the matter. My sweet Glenna will not be sacrificed to that devil. Mention it again and I'll be sore tempted to send you out to face the MacGregor in my place. Alone."

"Damn ye, Cameron. Your soft heart will be the death of us all."

There was a shuffling of feet, followed by heavy footsteps coming toward the door.

I scrambled back as quickly as I could, running to the end of the hall and around the corner on the balls of my feet so as not to make a sound. When I was safely out of sight, I swept my thick blonde hair back over my shoulder so that it would not be seen, and peered slowly around the corner. I watched my uncle's back disappear around the corner at the other end of the hall and gave out a relieved sigh.

I fell back against the cold stone wall and pressed the palm of my hand against the hammering beat of my heart. My mind was trying to reject what I had heard and yet I knew it to be true. Not only was the MacGregor heading for our lands, but my uncle wanted to offer me up to appease the warlord. While still innocent, I was no foolish young lass. I understood that my uncle meant to try to marry me off in an attempt to save our people. But to a murderer of men and a rapist of women? How little must he care for me to be so eager to condemn me to such a fate?

I hurried back to my room and locked the door once I was inside. My hunger was long forgotten as I crawled beneath the thick blankets on my bed. The half moon was high in the sky, and I stared at it, playing over and over again in my mind what I had just heard.

Even though I was scared, I knew that my father would keep me safe. Though my younger brother Fin would be the one to take over as clan chief after our father, I had always had a special place in his heart. So much so that he had even found me an English tutor to teach me languages and sums and soften my highland speech, just as his father had done for him. It was an unheard-of education for a young Scottish lass. I knew that his indulgence of me was the only reason I was still unwed at the age of five and twenty years.

If I had been any other woman, any hope of seeing me wed would have been lost long ago. But as the daughter of a highland chief I still held value, even if it was only my dowry that suitors found attractive. My father had indulged me by never forcing me to marry and allowing me to try to make a love match. But no man had yet been able to claim my heart. And if my uncle had his way, it looked as if for all my stubbornness on the matter, I would end up even worse off than I ever could have thought.

I sat at the breakfast table in my family's private dining room, staring forlornly at the eggs on my plate. My stomach had been tied in knots from the first moment

I had opened my eyes that morning and I could not bring myself to eat a single bite.

"Glenna, did you hear what I said?" my brother Fin asked me, tugging on my sleeve.

At twelve years old Fin was at that age where he was growing out of his childish ways, eager to become a man, but still had the fresh, precocious disposition of youth. What would become of him if the MacGregor were to take our lands?

"I'm sorry, Fin. I was over the hills and far away. What did you say?"

"I asked if you would come riding with me this afternoon. I want to go to the glen but I canna go alone. Oh, please say you'll come with me, Glenna. We can have a picnic," he pleaded.

I laughed and ruffled his dark hair. Finlay was my half brother, born of one of my father's serving ladies. My father, being the honorable man he is, had claimed Fin as his heir and moved his mother to a small, comfortable cottage on the lands where she would be able to live comfortably for the rest of her life.

Having spent so long as an only child, I had not been too pleased by the idea of having a little brother, but I had loved him from the first moment I set my eyes on his bright red face and thatch of dark hair as he waved his little fists and wailed lustily in my father's arms.

His cries had quieted the moment our father had

placed him in my hands, and I had sworn to be the best sister he could ever wish for.

"Of course we can, Fin. I'll see about getting a basket put together for our ride," I said, pushing past my worries to find a smile for him.

I could see our father watching us out of the corner of my eye. Worry lines were etched deep around the corners of his eyes as he studied me.

"Fin, lad. Give me a moment alone with your sister. We have a few things to be discussing this morning."

Fin looked back and forth between us and frowned. "Is Glenna in trouble?" he asked our father.

"No, lad, of course not. I just want to have a private word with her, is all. Run along, now. She'll find you when it's time to go to the stables."

Fin hesitated then threw his arms around me in a tight hug before leaving us.

I sat quietly with my head bowed and pushed the food around my plate.

"Now then, lass, why don't you tell me what's on your mind."

"It's nothing, Da. I just slept poorly, is all."

"Glenna, you've never slept poorly a day in your life. If you've started now, then something must be troubling you. I cannot help you unless you tell me what the problem is."

He sat back in his chair and waited patiently, watching me as I struggled to find the words.

I worried my lip, unsure of how much to tell him. If

I told him my fears about my uncle's plans for me, I would have to admit to eavesdropping on their conversation. I had been tossing and turning all night with worry.

"It's nothing, Father, truly. I was hungry last night, but too lazy to leave my bed. It must have affected my sleep, that's all. There's nothing more to it than that," I told him.

"All right then, lass, if you insist." He got up from his seat and came around the table to kiss the top of my head. "I'll leave you to your breakfast, then. I've a busy morning ahead of me."

Heavy footsteps entered the room and I froze at the sound of my uncle's voice.

"Are ye ready to go, Cameron?" my uncle asked my father.

"Yes, Dougal. I was just having a quick word with my daughter."

"Good morning, Glenna," my uncle said.

I turned stiffly in my chair to face him. His expression was blank as he looked at me and I wondered if even at that very moment his mind was scheming ways to convince my father to feed me to the MacGregor.

"Good morning, Uncle," I said coolly. "Did you sleep well?"

My uncle Dougal frowned at my tone, but did not remark on it.

"Yes, thank ye, Glenna. Now if ye don't mind, your

father and I have much to do today. Cameron?" With that, he turned and walked from the room.

"Have a good day, Glenna," my father said to me, patting me on the shoulder, "and be sure to actually put some of that in your mouth, aye?"

The moment I was alone I flopped back in my chair and sighed. I knew that my father would do everything he could to keep me out of the MacGregor's clutches. So why did I not feel more comforted by the thought?

CHAPTER 2

I leaned forward on my horse and laughed as I crested the hill in front of the keep. Looking back over my shoulder, I watched as my little brother urged his stallion faster, trying to keep up with me as we raced home.

"You'll have to do better than that if you plan on beating me one day, Fin!" I called back to him.

As we got closer to the castle I began to slow down, allowing Fin to close the gap and then pass me completely. He let out a cheer as he galloped past and crossed into the courtyard ahead of me.

It warmed my heart to watch him, and I grinned as he pulled back on the reins, bringing the horse to a stop, and jumped down.

"I beat you, Glenna! I knew I would!" he crowed.

"Aye, Fin, you did! And a mighty fine victory it was, too. Come, now, let's get the horses back to the stables and go wash up. And be sure to scrub under your fingernails unless you want Mrs. McNally to box your ears for you."

"Glenna, Fin, you must come quick!"

I turned from my brother to see Angus, my brother's sword instructor, rush into the courtyard toward us.

"What is it, Angus? We were just about to take the horses back to the stables," I told him.

"That can wait, lass. Your father is about to speak in the great hall. I was just headed out to fetch ye back to the keep. Come quickly, now, the both of ye. Someone else can see to the horses." He looked around the yard and called out to a young boy with bright red hair.

"You, there!" he called, getting the boy's attention. "Take these horses back to the stables. There's a good lad. Come on, now, the both of ye, follow me."

We followed Angus into the keep and he led us to the great hall. The room was so full that we had to shove our way through the crowd in order to reach the front where we would be able to see our father. People grumbled at first about being dislodged from their spots, but soon recognized us and shifted over to give us more room.

My father's eyes found mine and I nodded, wrapping an arm around my brother's shoulders. I knew what was coming. The troubled expression on my father's face and the deep lines in his brow gave it away long before he opened his mouth.

"News has come from the north." My father's booming voice filled the rafters of the great hall and we all listened intently.

"We have been warned that clan MacGregor plans to move against us within the week," he continued.

The room erupted into chaos at his words, with everyone shouting and talking over each other.

"Quiet, everyone. Quiet down, all of you!" he hollered, raising his hands in the air to regain our attention. "I'll thank you all to stay calm. Women and children are to stay inside the keep. Scouts will be sent out night and day to alert of us any sign of their approach."

"How do they expect to see the devil himself coming for them?" a man's voice called out.

"The MacGregor is not the devil. He is a man. He bleeds like a man and he will die like a man," my father said to the room.

"What of the wolves he commands?" cried a woman. "Giant beasts, unnatural. The hounds of hell!"

"If these hounds come for us, then your men of clan Gordon will send them back to the pits they came from. Them and the man who commands them. We will not be cowed. We will not quake in fear behind our walls. We are Gordons!" he boomed.

"We are Gordons!" the room yelled back.

When the announcement was finished my brother and I hurried up to the dais, where our father pulled me in for a tight hug and squeezed Fin's shoulder. Even though I still had the tendency to treat Fin like a boy, our father treated him more like a young man. With my mother long dead and Fin's mother no longer in the keep, I felt like between my father and I it gave my brother some balance. I didn't want him to grow up too quickly, but it would do him no good to grow up soft either.

"I want you two to be sticking close to home from now on, understand?"

"Yes, Da." I nodded my head in agreement.

Fin scowled up at him, putting on his bravest face. "I don't want to hide in the keep with the women and children, Da. I want to help the men. I can protect our home with you and the others. I've gotten good with a sword. Even Angus says so. Just ask him."

"I know you want to help me protect your sister and the others, lad, but I need you to stay safe. You're my heir, Fin, and for all you're growing into a fine young man, it's not yet time for you to see your first battle or to spill a man's blood. No, do as I say and stay within the walls."

"But, Da—"

"The answer is no, Finlay," he said firmly.

"Come on, now, Fin," I said to my brother. "Our father has a lot to do. We shouldn't be taking up all of his time. There are a lot of people who will be needing to speak to him. We'll find him again later."

I tugged on my brother's arm until he followed me from the hall and back to our rooms.

In every corner of the keep people were huddled together, speculating in hushed voices about the future of our clan. I walked faster and tried to block them out, praying that my father had a plan.

Tensions were high in the hall at dinner that night. I sat at the head table with my family and looked out across the room. The only smiles I saw were those on the faces of children too young yet to understand the danger that was headed their way.

Normally at dinner the hall was filled with laughter and cheer, music, or even a story or two if a traveling entertainer happened to be passing through our lands. But instead the air was filled with only the noise of stressed whispers and the scraping of plates.

My father and uncle seemed to have had another disagreement over something. Neither one of them was speaking to the other. Instead they chose to keep their eyes focused on the food in front of them. It was unlike them not to show a united front to our clansmen, and I worried that their obvious discord would only heighten the fear of our people.

I shifted uncomfortably, feeling the weight of my uncle's gaze on me. I doubted that Father had convinced him to give up on his plans for me so quickly. It was the only reason why they would still be so angry at one another.

I turned to my uncle and caught his eye, then raised my eyebrows at him in a questioning stare.

He glared at me, then hastily returned his eyes to his plate. There was now no doubt in my mind. My uncle still believed that the only way to help our people was to hand me over to the MacGregor, but it didn't matter so long as my father stood opposed. I turned back to my meal and finished eating in silence along with the rest of my family, then went to bed early. I was more than ready for the start of a new day.

CHAPTER 3

y eyes flew open, awakened from sleep by the weight of someone's hand pressed firmly across my mouth. A large, hooded figure hovered over my bed, his face hidden in the shadows, and I lashed out in fear. With my fingers curled, I raked my nails down the back of the intruder's hand, but when it wouldn't budge I went for his eyes instead, resulting in a swift backhand to my face.

"Glenna, get a hold of yourself, lass. It's me, Dougal," my uncle's voice hissed in annoyance. He removed his hand from my mouth and I scooted up the bed, pressing myself back against the headboard, trying to put as much space between us as possible.

"Uncle? What do you think you're doing, sneaking into my room like this is the middle of the night and scaring me half to death? You hit me!" I raised my hand to the warm spot on my cheek.

"Aye, I'm sorry about that. I just needed to stop ye before ye blinded me. You'll notice that I dinna actually strike ye that hard."

Now that the shock had passed I realized he was right. My face didn't actually hurt very much.

"What are you doing in here?" I hissed.

"I'm to take ye out of the castle, lass. You're to be kept somewhere safe until all the fighting is over to make sure that the MacDougal cannot get his hands on you."

I hesitated and eyed him suspiciously.

"Why did my father not come for me himself?" I asked my uncle.

"Because he is seeing to young Finlay."

"Are my brother and I not to go together, then?" My heart plummeted at the thought of being separated from my brother for an unknown amount of time.

"We thought it best not to have the two of ye hidden together. In the chance that you're found, it would do no good to have both children of the Gordon in one place."

His explanation made sense and my doubts started to subside.

"All right," I told him at last. "What will I need?"

"Just get yourself dressed and find a good cloak. We must be leaving at once. I'll wait outside your door for you."

Once the door was closed I jumped out of bed and searched in the wardrobe for my dark green gown.

Simple in design and made of serviceable fabric, it was perfectly suited for a rough journey and seemed my best choice, as I had no idea how long I would be gone for. I tidied my hair into one long plait down my back and slipped my feet into my sturdy leather riding boots, moving as fast as possible so as not to keep my uncle waiting.

I pulled my hood up over my head to cloak my face and stepped out into the hall where my uncle was waiting. Silently, we made our way through the keep, watching carefully to avoid anyone who might be wandering the halls. No one was to know that I was leaving.

In the courtyard a lone clansman stood waiting for us, holding the reins of a single horse. The hood of his cloak was pulled down low over his face, making him unrecognizable, and he did not say a word when he helped me up into the saddle before disappearing into the shadows. Dougal mounted the horse behind me and took the reins, inching the horse closer to the gates.

The courtyard gates swung open just wide enough for the horse to slip through, and then we were off, galloping into the night.

Dougal still had not told me where it was he was taking me, but wherever it was, I knew that he wouldn't be staying with me. My father would need him back at the keep to help lead the men when the MacGregor attacked.

I closed my eyes and prayed for the safety of not only my father and brother, but for every one of our clansmen, the people in the castle and throughout our lands, that they would be protected from the terrors of the MacGregor and his hellhounds. I felt as if I were abandoning them, my escape an act of cowardice. But if I were captured I could be ransomed, or worse. And if Finlay were to be killed it would be a great blow to the clan Gordon.

No, leaving was best, even if it did put a sour taste in my mouth.

After riding in silence for hours my curiosity finally got the best of me and I decided to risk my uncle's annoyance.

"Where is it that you're taking me, Uncle?"

"Somewhere you'll be safe," he said simply.

"But where is that? Am I to be the guest of one of the neighboring lairds?"

"Aye, lass, ye are, but I'll not be telling ye which one."

"Why not? Don't I have the right to know who my host will be for the foreseeable future?" I asked with a huff. I had so little say in what was happening to me, I didn't appreciate being treated like a child as well.

"It's for your own safety, lass. The less ye know, the better off you'll be, believe me. These are dangerous times."

"It's always dangerous times, Uncle, when the MacGregor men are roaming the highlands," I said testily.

"Then ye should know better than to be asking me silly questions," he snapped.

I fell silent, stung by his words. I fought the urge to let loose my tongue and speak my mind on the matter, but it would do me no good in any event. If he was determined not to tell me the details of our journey, then no amount of pestering him on my part would loosen his tongue on the matter.

But a kernel of disquiet was growing within me. A small doubt nagging at the back of my mind.

"I want to go back," I told him.

"What are ye on about now, lass? Ye know we can't go back. There is not enough time."

"I want to go back, Uncle. I want to speak to my father. I have to hear it from him myself that this is what he wants."

"Did I not tell ye that this is what he wants? Is my word not good enough for ye now, then? Do you not trust me, Glenna, your own uncle?"

I realized then that I didn't trust him. I didn't trust a single word he had said to me that night.

"We're going back," I said, jerking hard on the reins he held.

The horse let out a loud whinny and kicked out at the air in front of it.

"Ye stupid girl!" my uncle yelled, fighting to get the stallion back under control.

He shoved me off of the horse and I landed hard in the dirt with the breath knocked out of me. Gasping for breath, I struggled to crawl away, but my uncle came up behind me and roughly rolled me over.

"My soft fool of a brother allowed ye too much freedom," he snarled as he grabbed my hands and bound my wrists in front of me. "Now ye can finally be of some use."

"You will never get away with this," I gasped, the air slowly making its way back into my lungs.

"And you, my dear niece, are to be seen and not heard," he said, shoving a rag into my mouth.

I struggled against him as he hauled me off the ground, but he overpowered me and placed me back onto the horse.

"Try anything stupid like that again and you'll regret it."

We rode for three days and three nights, stopping to rest only when the sun rose above the horizon, then setting out again when it began to set. Dougal seldom stuck to the main roads, choosing instead to lead the horse along the edges of the trees where he could keep an eye out for other travelers. He kept me bound and gagged so that I could neither escape nor cry out for help. With every passing hour my heart sank lower, knowing that soon any sliver of hope I held for being found on the road would soon be crushed by the hands of the MacGregor.

The sun was long set on the day as Dougal guided our horse carefully through the forest with only the moon to guide the way. Obscured in a cloudy sky, its light filtered down through the thick branches of the trees around us.

Dougal sat tense in the saddle behind me. Every so often he would stop the horse and cock his head, listening hard for something in the distance.

It was on one of these stops that I heard it: voices off in the trees. I was sure that Dougal would turn the horse to give us a wide berth around the group and was shocked when he headed straight in that direction. This couldn't be where he was taking me, I thought. It was too soon.

Soon the voices grew more distinct, and the bright glow of a fire could be made out between the trees. As we got closer to the camp I shifted uncomfortably. There was a strange prickling sensation between my shoulder blades, as if we were being watched. I peered into the darkness, but could not see anyone there. Looking back at Dougal I could see that his mouth was set in a thin line as he continued to ride with an uncharacteristic stiffness, as if waiting for an attack.

"I'm thinking that will be about far enough for the both of you."

We were still a ways off from the fire when a deep voice called out to us, and Dougal brought the stallion to a halt.

I could not see which one of the men had spoken, but all of the other voices quieted at his announcement.

Dougal climbed down off the horse and then pulled me down, keeping a hand firmly on my arm.

"I seek an audience with the leader of this group," Dougal told them, his voice loud and clear.

"And why would he be bothering to speak to ye?" the voice asked us.

Dougal brought us a few feet closer still, never releasing me from his grasp.

"Because I have something of great import to discuss with him. All I need is a moment of his time."

The horse whinnied behind me, drawing my attention. When I looked over my shoulder there were men coming out of the trees behind us, closing us in.

"Bring them to me," a voice by the fire called out, and the men advanced on us.

In my fright I stumbled and clutched at my uncle as the men herded us closer to the fire and the voice of authority.

As we came into the circle of firelight I looked around to see men sprawled in the small clearing, about fifteen of them in total, not counting the men who were still behind us in the shadows of the trees.

These were the men who were going to decimate our lands? My mind raced with confusion. There was nothing more than a handful of men here. This was no great army. The messenger must have gotten it wrong. MacGregors or no, my father's men would have easily been able to stop a group this small. Unless they hadn't planned on attacking us, and my uncle had known that all along.

As I examined them they looked back at us with expressions ranging from mild amusement to outright suspicion.

"Which one of you is the man I seek?" Dougal asked them, pulling himself up to his full height.

The men broke out into raucous laughter, but no one stepped forward.

A hunched figure was sitting directly across the fire from us with his head low down by his knees, making it impossible to see his face. My stomach knotted tightly at the sight of him. I couldn't explain how I knew, but something inside of me told me that this was the man who had spoken before.

"I am Dougal Gordon, brother of Cameron Gordon, the chief of Clan Gordon, and I demand to speak with your leader."

"You're a brave man to be making demands of us here tonight." The voice came to us again, and this time I had no doubt in my mind that it came from the hunched figure across from us.

The head lifted and bright eyes the color of emeralds met mine. The light of the fire was reflected in them, making them dance and sparkle in a hard face framed by long black hair that fell to his shoulders.

I stood completely frozen in his gaze, and he didn't speak again for a long moment as his eyes stared into mine. I swallowed behind my gag and broke out into a cold sweat. He was the most striking man I had ever seen, and the most fearsome.

Very slowly, he rose from his spot by the fire and my eyes went wide as my head tilted back to look at him. He was a giant, taller than me by at least a foot. His broad shoulders and chest tapered into a trim waist. His kilt ended at the knee, revealing thick, muscular calves. I swallowed, resisting the urge to take a step back in retreat.

"So tell me then, Dougal Gordon, what brings you here to make demands of the MacGregor?"

Terror clawed up inside of me and pushed me to action. I tore my arm out of my uncle's grip and ran blindly for the trees. Blood pounded in my ears and I had only made it a few steps before my uncle's arm wrapped around my waist and he hauled me back to the fire pit.

"No!" I screamed, but it was muffled by the gag. I kicked out wildly and struggled against his grip.

"Shut up, ye stupid girl. It's the only way."

I screamed at the top of my lungs and he clamped a hand over my mouth, forcing the gag in deeper. I choked on the taste of sweat, dirt and leather.

Through my panic I could see the MacGregor watching us with an expression of faint interest, but he said nothing.

"MacGregor. I bring you Glenna Gordon, eldest

child and only daughter of chief Cameron Gordon," Dougal told him.

"The lass doesn't look to be very happy to be making my acquaintance. Why don't ye tell me why you've brought her here?"

I strained against Dougal's grip, but he refused to release me. His arms were tight across my ribcage, keeping me trapped.

"We got word that your men were soon to be on our lands. The Gordon wants no trouble from you, MacGregor. His daughter is a peace offering. Leave our lands be and she is yours."

Furious with what I was hearing, I reached up and dug my nails into the flesh on the back of my uncle's hand, then ripped down as hard as I could.

"Ye wee bitch!" he spat, yanking his hand away and shoving me away from him.

I fell into the dirt on my hands and knees, just barely missing the fire. I used my few precious moments of freedom to tear the gag out of my mouth.

"My father will have your head for this!" I shouted. "The devil take you, Uncle. You'll never get away with this."

"And just what do ye expect me to do with her, Dougal?"

The MacGregor did not even bother to glance in my direction, completely ignoring my outburst as if I had not spoken.

"It matters not to me. Take her to your bed or put

her to work. Do with her as you please. Just leave our lands in peace."

"And what if me and my men think we would find more pleasure in stealing your cattle and taking what we choose? Or gathering my forces and decimating your lands? I have no need of her."

The MacGregor looked down at me with narrow eyes. I felt as if he looked straight into the core of me, burning through me in an attempt to see all that I was. I could not have felt more exposed if I had been standing there before him in naught but my shift.

"Damn ye, MacGregor. Is your heart truly so black? Maybe ye really are the devil, as they say," Dougal spat.

The MacGregor's bright green eyes flashed in anger and he took a step forward. The fire was the only thing separating him and my uncle, and I was sure it was the only thing that kept my uncle from losing his head in that very moment. I was almost sorry that it barred the giant man's path, so angry was I at this betrayal by my own blood.

"Take her." The MacGregor's command was devoid of all emotion.

Two of his men advanced on me and I swung out wildly with my bound hands, trying to fend them off as they hauled me to my feet and dragged me off to the side.

"I'll take what you've offered. And I may or may not leave your lands and your people in peace. I make ye no promises. But ye have my word that I'll let ye leave our camp alive if ye go now and do not look back. That's my offer. The girl for your life. Take it or leave it."

"I want your word, MacGregor, that you'll not savage our land," Dougal said, enraged, his face going bright red.

"The only word you'll have from me is for my men to separate your head from your shoulders if ye do not leave this place at once," the MacGregor said coolly.

My uncle looked at him with naked fury in his eyes. He opened his mouth then closed it again, apparently thinking better about what he had been about to say, and turned his back on us without a single glance in my direction.

"Uncle, you cannot do this to me. Please, please don't do this," I begged him, hot tears running down my face.

But he did not come back for me. Abandoned and surrounded by the men of clan MacGregor, I wept hot tears, terrified of the fate that lay ahead of me.

CHAPTER 4

"Watch her," MacGregor told his men, "and do something to quiet her. I don't want to have to listen to her weeping the entire night while I'm trying to sleep."

Taking hold of my elbow, they pulled me toward the fire, then shoved me down onto one of the logs they had placed there to sit on.

"Now keep quiet," one of them growled at me. "Unless ye want your noise to be bringing the MacGregor over here to quiet ye down himself."

"Who knows," the other one said with a sneer. "Maybe she would."

They sat down on either side of me, laughing at their distasteful joke, then proceeded to ignore me completely. All of the men went back to their drinking and conversation as if the interruption had never happened.

I shifted uncomfortably on the log and my stomach let out a loud rumble. My face flushed warmly as every set of eyes turned to look at me. How could they all have possibly heard the noise I had made from so far away?

The eyes of the men across from me shifted to look over my shoulder and I heard heavy footsteps coming up behind me. I did not need to turn around to know who it was. I could sense the MacGregor's eyes on the back of my head and I tensed up in fear.

A large hand reached over my shoulder and dropped a large hunk of bread in my lap.

"Eat." The MacGregor's command was simple. I hesitated for a moment, unsure if it was some sort of cruel joke, then snatched up the food and took a large bite before he had the chance to take it away from me again.

I ate the bread quickly, not knowing when the next time they chose to feed me would be. The clansman to my right shifted and bumped into me, causing me to swallow wrong, and I began to choke.

I coughed and struggled to swallow it down, but it was lodged too thickly. I doubled over, trying to loosen it, but the piece would not move.

"What's wrong with her?" someone asked.

I grabbed the shoulder of the man to my right, clutching at his shirtsleeve.

"Christ, she's choking!" he shouted, then turned me away from him and pounded me on the back.

The chunk of bread dislodged itself from my throat and I spat it out into the fire then fell backward off the log into the dirt, gasping for breath as I curled myself up into a ball.

"Is she all right?"

"Jesus, she's pale."

"Look at her hands. Her fingers are turning blue."

Out of the confusion of voices around me one voice rang clear. His.

"I told ye to watch her, not kill or cripple her," the MacGregor said.

I felt the rope around my wrists slacken then give way. I lay completely still, then peeked through my semi-closed eyes to see that only one man was bending over me now. Moving quickly, I grabbed a fair-sized rock and swung for him, hitting him with it as hard as I could on the side of the head. I scrambled to my feet, taking advantage of the momentary confusion, and ran for the trees as fast as I could.

I heard the shouts of the men behind me, but it only helped to spur me on. I didn't look back to see how many of them were following me; I couldn't risk wasting the precious seconds that it would take.

It took me a long while to realize that no one was chasing me. I heard no shouting, no footsteps, nothing but the sound of my own ragged breathing in my ears.

I slowed, then came to a complete stop. Something wasn't right. Why would they just let me escape?

Then I heard it. A snapping in the trees. I spun

around in a circle, trying to find the direction it was coming from. A low growl reached me and I took a step back, my heart pounding loudly in my chest.

The howl of a wolf went up in the night and I took off blindly, deeper into the woods. The sound of crashing came from behind me and I cried out, my lungs burning from the exertion.

The hem of my gown got caught on a bush and I went crashing to the ground. I hissed at the burning on the palms of my hands as they got scratched up on the twigs and rocks that littered the forest floor.

I shook with terror, listening to the sound of breaking branches. It took all of my courage to bring myself to turn around and face whatever it was that was stalking me. My nightmare came rushing back to me in a blinding flash. The blood-covered snow. The bright amber eyes.

I pulled myself up and looked over my shoulder to face the largest, most terrifying beast I had ever laid my eyes on.

I couldn't even scream, I was so petrified with fear. The giant wolf stalked toward me, head low to the ground, with its large golden eyes fixed on mine.

I knew all too well the stories told about the demon wolves that Alastair MacGregor called forth to do his bidding. I had never fully believed them, sure that they were just the stories told by the scared and confused survivors of his bloodthirsty raids. But I could not deny what I was seeing with my own eyes.

My father had always told me that it was men that had killed my mother. Killed her, but had left me alive. That my nightmare was just my child's mind turning the men into monsters. But now I knew the truth. The wolf had been real.

The giant wolf circled me. I watched it carefully, afraid that it would lunge and attack me at any moment, but it did not. Instead it moved closer, bringing its circles ever so slowly tighter until it was so close that I could have reached out my hand and touched it if I had been so bold.

It moved behind me, and I felt the great beast press its muzzle against my back and nudge me. I jumped and let out a whimper but did not move, just sat shaking with fright. It nudged at my back again, more firmly this time, and I jumped to my feet, moving quickly to get away from it.

It stepped toward me and I moved a few feet back, then stopped. The wolf stepped toward me again and I knew I had no choice but to turn around and walk back to the MacGregor camp. The wolf was to be my escort.

It was no wonder none of the men had bothered to chase me themselves. They knew that I would be found and brought back to them in time.

The wolf followed closely behind me, its inky black coat melting in and out of the shadows, but never moved to attack. The MacGregor really was some sort of devil if he had such command over a beast of this kind. It was the only way to explain how a wolf of this size had never been spotted anywhere but at the call of the MacGregor clan.

It was not just the current clan chief who was said to have the power over the demon wolves, but all of the chiefs for as far back as anyone could remember. There had always been stories, legends, about the clan's protectors.

The light from the fire pit was soon within view and I stopped walking. Maybe it was because I had been in the presence of one of these great beasts twice now and survived, but after my experience in the woods and the hike back in the company of the giant wolf, I was more afraid of the men than I was of the beast.

The wolf stopped beside me and turned to look at me, piercing me with its golden gaze, then looked back at the camp through the trees.

"I cannot," I whispered, my voice shaking with fear and anger. "I cannot go back there to be beaten or face whatever punishment the devil MacGregor has in store for me for trying to escape." I faced the wolf and lifted my head, squaring my shoulders. "You may as well tear my throat out now."

I don't know what made me think that the beast would be able to understand me, but I could not keep my feelings inside.

"Please, please, don't make me go," I begged.

The beast shoved me toward the camp with its great

head, and I balled my hands into fists. Of course it couldn't understand me. And even if it could, why would I think that my pleading would do me any kind of good?

Well, I was no coward. I was the daughter of Cameron Gordon, and I would meet my fate with the dignity of my rank.

The wolf melted back into the trees, but I was not so foolish as to think that I was being allowed a chance to escape. No, if anything the beast most likely sensed my resignation.

I stepped out of the trees into the light of the campfire and the voices hushed at my approach.

With great dignity I walked over to the fire, looking each and every man dead in the eye before taking up a position close to the flames.

The MacGregor was not among those I saw there, but I knew that I would be seeing him soon enough. And then I would have to accept my punishment. I was determined that no matter what he did to me, he would not see a single tear or hear one whimper. I would not give him the satisfaction.

A few minutes later I looked up to see the MacGregor walking out of the trees. Our eyes met across the fire and I clenched my hands in the folds of my dress to keep them from shaking.

"Callum," he called to one of the men, his eyes never leaving mine. "You're next on watch."

Out of the corner of my eye I could see a young

man who looked no older than sixteen stand up and head off into the woods.

Once he was gone, the MacGregor pulled his gaze from mine and turned and walked away.

I sat there in confusion. Was I not to be punished after all, or was I to be punished later?

"Come on, then, lass," said the clansman next to me.

The man was older than my father. His barrel chest made him look broad and strong even though his dark, wiry hair and thick, bushy beard were generously streaked with gray.

"It's getting late and we've an early start tomorrow. It's best ye get some sleep."

I looked around and noticed that everyone was starting to bed down for the night.

"Lay yourself down. You've had more than enough adventure for one day."

"I don't think I could sleep at all tonight," I whispered.

"Ye feel that way now, but close your eyes and I'd be surprised if ye were still awake after five minutes."

I narrowed my eyes at him and crossed my arms over my chest. "Why are you being so nice to me?"

"Because ye look like you could use it, lass," he told me, then wrapped himself in his plaid, lay down on the ground and closed his eyes.

I stared at him for a moment, caught off guard by his show of kindness, then decided to take his advice.

The ground was hard but warm, being so close to the fire. Curling myself into a tight ball, I closed my eyes and quickly fell asleep.

CHAPTER 5

*L*arge hands shook me roughly awake by my shoulders. It took a moment for the memory of where I was to come back to me in the low light of the morning. My exhaustion had put me into a deep, dreamless sleep, and my mind fought against leaving that peaceful world.

A man came over and doused the fire that the sentries had kept burning throughout the night, and I watched as a thick cloud of smoke curled up toward the sky.

I had been gone for four nights. And while I wanted to believe that my father and his men were out looking for me at that very moment, I knew that my uncle would have found some way to keep my father pacified during my absence. Some sort of explanation that would keep him from coming to look for me before my uncle could get back to our land and whisper some sort of clever lie in his ear.

"Time to wake up now, lass," said the older man who'd been kind to me the night before. He stood up and took hold of the reins of the horse he had led over. "We're heading out and you're to be riding with the MacGregor. Best not to keep him waiting."

He held out his hand to me and I accepted it graciously, allowing him to pull me to my feet.

"I don't suppose I have time to..." I trailed off, blushing, and looked into the woods.

"Aye, come along, then. It will be a long ride once we get going. Best ye go now."

He stood watch with his back turned while I relieved myself in the trees, then walked me back to the camp.

"Where are we going?" I asked him.

"We're just off to do a wee bit o' reiving, that's all. Nothing for you to fash yourself about."

I didn't know how he could think that being stuck with them while they stole livestock in the middle of the night wouldn't frighten me. Reiving was common practice in the highlands, and in a few years even Fin would be getting his first taste of it along with the other young men. But it was one thing to know it was happening, and another altogether to be dragged into the middle of it against your will.

In the full light of day the MacGregor looked just as fearsome as he had the night before. He stood unsmiling alongside his great black mount with annoyance in his eyes. He had obviously been waiting for me and I picked up my pace to reach him.

"Donald, did you not tell the lass that we have not got all day?" he asked the older man.

"Aye, I did. And she's here now, so ye can quit your grumbling," Donald told him.

I looked agape at the older man, amazed that he would dare take such a tone with his chief, especially one with such a reputation.

The MacGregor simply grunted and held out his hand to me, then helped me up into the saddle, leaving Donald to watch me while he oversaw the last details before it was time to move out. The thought of attempting to escape now that I sat a horse passed through my mind, but the thought was fleeting. I doubted I would get very far, or that the MacGregor would be as forgiving a second time.

It wasn't long before every man was packed up and mounted, ready to set off, and the MacGregor swung himself up into the saddle behind me in one smooth motion. Settling himself, he took up the reins in one hand and held me firmly with the other, his strong arm wrapped tightly around my waist.

We rode all day, with the men talking and laughing amongst themselves. Ribald jokes were tossed back and forth between them and I found it hard to reconcile the thought of the men around me being capable of all the monstrous things I had heard about in the stories. Was it really so easy for them to go from singing and laughter to destroying lives as if they were nothing?

The MacGregor shifted in the saddle behind me and I was once again pulled from my thoughts. I had not been able to keep my mind focused for more that a few scant minutes at a time all day. Too easily I would find my awareness drawn back to the feel of his hard, broad chest against my back, or the feel of his long, muscular thighs as they pressed up alongside my own.

But the worst, the very worst, was when his hand would move slightly and slide along my abdomen as if in a caress. Every time it happened I could feel a heat begin to pool in the very center of me and it would take all of my determination not to close my eyes and lean back against him.

How wanton I must truly be to crave the touch of such a man. The knowledge of my desire shamed me to my very core and I rode in silence, only opening my mouth to eat the food that was shared with me on our journey.

It was full night by the time we had reached our destination. The air of the group had changed from lighthearted fun to a more serious tone the closer we got to the impending rieving.

The band of men kept their horses in a tight circle as we waited for the scout to come back. The

MacGregor had sent young Callum ahead of us to scout the land.

"Where are we?" I whispered to Donald, too curious to keep quiet any longer. We had ridden all day and I was eager to finally have a moment to stretch my legs.

"We've passed into Boyle lands. It won't be long now," he told me.

He was right. About fifteen minutes later, Callum came back creeping through the trees and headed straight for the MacGregor to give him the report.

"There is a small cluster of homes just down the hill. A bit of livestock. A couple of horses, a few cows, the usual chickens. Not much to pick from," Callum told him, loud enough for the rest of us to hear.

"That'll be serving our purposes just fine. Ye all know the plan. Get in, get out."

I watched as a few of the men ran into the trees in different directions and disappeared.

"Donald," he called, beckoning him over.

"Aye." Donald nodded to me and we walked over to the MacGregor.

I kept my head down and tried to partially shield myself with Donald's frame but he held on to me tightly and kept me firmly in view. I tried not to be resentful as the man had shown me nothing but kindness, but I still found myself annoyed that he would put me back in the line of the MacGregor's attentions. These last few minutes with some distance between us had been the first time all day where I had felt like I could take a breath without being consumed by the scent and feel of him.

"Keep to the edge of the trees and watch for us. I want ye to stay back this time and keep an eye on the lass. I'm counting on ye to mind her. The last thing we need is her getting free and having to fetch her back again."

Even if I had been thinking of using this time to try to make my escape, the reminder of what he would send to collect me would have been more than enough to ensure I stayed put.

"Not to worry," Donald told him. "I don't think she plans on giving us any trouble, do ye, lass?"

I kept my eyes averted and shook my head.

The MacGregor reached out and took my face in his hands, raising it so that I had to look him in the eye.

"Look at me, lass," he said.

I slowly raised my eyes to meet his.

"Don't do anything foolish," he told me very slowly.

I swallowed and nodded my head. The skin on my face felt like it was burning at his touch. "I won't," I whispered.

He released me and walked away from us without another word.

Donald and I stood quietly at the edge of the trees and watched as the men crept down toward the small grouping of houses below. Once they reached the homes, they dashed in and out of the shadows, heading for the barn.

It wasn't long before I noticed that another shape had joined the men in the dark, and I gasped when I realized that giant wolves were with them. With their large jaws wrapped around fence posts, they tore down parts of the small garden fences and trampled the edges around the vegetables. It took me a moment to realize that they weren't actually doing any real harm to the crops themselves.

Soon they were scratching at the doors of the houses and sending up loud howls, which seemed to signal to the men that it was time to fall back.

The men came running back into the trees, two of them leading horses and yelling the MacGregor clan war cry into the night. They wasted no time mounting their horses and taking off into the woods at top speed with their spoils.

"Come along, now. It's time to go," Donald told me, tugging on my arm.

I hurried with him over to our horse and let him boost me up into the seat. Soon we were off with the rest of them, galloping away from the Boyle crofting as fast as we could.

My mind swirled with confusion as we raced through the night. There had been no violence, no fires, no death and only minor damage done. Where were the bloody beatings I had been warned about? No wives or daughters had been dragged from their beds to slake the craven lust of these MacGregor men. It was not at all what I had been expecting, what I had been warned about my entire life.

Even my own treatment at the hands of these men had not been wholly unpleasant. I suddenly wondered if any of us really knew who these people were, these men of clan MacGregor.

CHAPTER 6

A few days later we arrived at Meggernie Castle, nestled in the center of the beautiful valley of Glen Lyon. The tired and dirty men sent up a cheer as their home came into view, eager to get back behind the magnificent castle's walls.

I, on the other hand, was filled with trepidation. On the other side of those gates, a whole new life was waiting for me, and I had yet to be told exactly what would be expected of me. The circumstances of my situation meant that I could not expect to be treated as a political guest here. I was not wed to the MacGregor but was in fact a hostage, which meant that I could be tossed in irons and locked away at his whim. Especially since none of my clan knew where I was, or had the ability to visit to ensure that my treatment was befitting of my rank.

My uncle had tossed me at the MacGregor's feet with permission to do what he would with me. And no matter their decent treatment of me up to this point; nothing was guaranteed until the terms of my capture were officially laid out.

We dismounted from our horses and handed them off to the grooms who greeted us at the castle doors. I took a deep breath and held my head high in the face of all the people who had come out to see their chief and his men safely home.

"Donald, bring her," said the MacGregor in a clipped tone as he led us into the keep.

I followed him through the halls of the keep with Donald following close on my heels, ignoring the curious looks of the castle occupants as we passed.

I was led to a large study which boasted a fireplace as tall as a man with two large leather chairs pulled up in front of it. On one side was a large bookcase, and the center of the room was dominated by a large desk, which the MacGregor moved to stand behind.

"Thank you, Donald. You can leave us now."

I turned around to look at Donald, shooting him a pleading look. I was not ready to be left alone with this terrifying man.

"Don't worry, lass, you'll be just fine," Donald said to me. He stepped forward and gave my hand a quick squeeze before exiting the study and closing the door behind him.

"Take a seat, Glenna Gordon. There's much we need to be discussing."

A shiver went down my spine at the sound of his deep voice. It felt strange to hear my name on his lips, but not unpleasant.

He waited until I had arranged myself in the seat across from his great desk before sitting himself. Leaning back in his chair, he studied me quietly for so long that I began to shift uncomfortably under his scrutiny.

"How did you come to be here, lass?" he asked suddenly.

"You know that as well as I. My traitorous uncle handed me over to you."

"Yes, but I'm still not sure I believe his reason why."

I couldn't believe what I was hearing. Was there really any doubt in his mind about the lengths a desperate man would go to when faced with the idea of dealing with the infamous highland chief?

"My uncle wanted to ensure that you would leave our people in peace. He believed that handing me over to you was the only way that peace could be guaranteed."

"And ye know this for certain, then, do ye? How do ye know that it's not some part of a larger plot?" He leaned forward over the desk and looked me in the eye. "How can I even be certain that ye are who ye say ye are? Ye could be a serving wench for all I know."

I bristled at the accusation, my back going stiff.

"How dare you, sir. You sit there and accuse me of being a liar after all that I've been through? Dragged from my bed. Bound and gagged by my own blood. Dragged through the forest for three nights and three days only to be thrown down at the feet of the dreaded highland chief Alastair MacGregor, he who has the very hounds of hell at his command. What exactly do you think I would have to gain from putting myself in such a precarious position? I am Glenna Gordon, daughter of Cameron Gordon, and I will not have my word on the matter doubted again."

By now I was out of my seat and looking down at him, my chest rising and falling rapidly in my ire. When I had finished speaking and had started to calm down, my ire turned to shock and then fear. I had always been known for speaking my mind, but to lose my temper with such a man was beyond stupidity.

"I'm sorry," I said quietly, gripping the arms of the chair so tightly that my knuckles turned white and lowering myself back into my seat. "The stress of the last week seems to have gotten the better of me."

"No serving wench, even one sent here as a spy, would have had the nerve to give me the sharp edge of her tongue. If anything, your outburst has proved what no amount of pretty words could have, Glenna Gordon."

I closed my eyes and sighed in relief, easing my grip on the chair.

"What is to become of me?" I asked quietly.

"Your uncle has used ye to buy the safety of the Gordon lands. In order for that agreement to be honored, you have no other choice but to stay here with me."

"B-but," I stuttered, "my uncle does not have that authority. My father never would have allowed this deal to be struck. I heard him myself. He was wholly against it."

"Would ye prefer I reject the offer and march against your people?" He sat back in his chair and raised his eyebrows at me, his long fingers steepled under his chin.

"No!" I shouted, appalled at the prospect.

"Then it comes down to this, lass. If ye agree to stay here with me, then I will consider the deal a binding contract. The Gordons will have nothing more to fear from the clan MacGregor. But if you say nay, then you leave your clan open to further attack. The choice is yours."

I sat frozen, deaf to all but the sound of my beating heart echoing in my ears. I had no choice. What was the worth of my freedom if it meant putting my entire clan in danger? Could I give up my future, my family, my freedom, if it meant that my clan no longer had to fear this man?

"I'll stay," I whispered.

He nodded and stood, then walked around the desk toward me. "I'll show ye to your chamber."

He held out his hand to me and after a moment of hesitation I slipped my hand into his. A spark went through my hand at the contact and I started to pull my hand back, but he closed his fingers around mine and placed my hand on his arm, then escorted me from the room.

CHAPTER 7

I did not go downstairs to the great hall for dinner that night, choosing instead to spend the evening in solitude, isolated in my new room. My chamber was large and comfortable, dominated on one side by a giant bed, piled high with pillows and furs to ward off the chill in the night air. It also boasted a fireplace, though not as large as the one in the study downstairs. There was a sitting area with a large window and a table with a cushioned stool where I could sit to have my hair dressed in the mornings, as well as a large tub for bathing behind a screen. The perfect gilded cage.

I was sitting in one of the twin chairs by the window, staring out over the large lush grounds behind the castle, my heart aching for home, when I heard a strange shuffling outside my chamber.

I crossed the room and pressed my ear to the door,

but the sound had stopped. Taking hold of the handle, I tugged lightly on the door and gasped in surprise to find it unlocked. Easing it open, I looked down to see the form of the great black wolf lying across my doorway. I knew in an instant that it was the same beast that had been sent to bring me back to the camp when I had attempted to escape.

The wolf's ears perked up and it turned to look at me, fixing me with its great golden-eyed stare. I swallowed and tried to calm the rapid beating of my heart.

"Are you to keep me from escaping, then?" I asked the wolf, my voice shaking. "Well, you can tell the MacGregor that I have every intention of keeping my word. I am not about to risk the safety of my people. And tell him... tell him that he can go right to the devil," I snapped, and slammed the door closed.

The next morning I did not go downstairs for breakfast. I was not ready to face the stares, or speak to anyone. I preferred my isolation.

Come lunch time there was a knock on my door. I looked up just as the MacGregor stormed into the room, his face red with anger.

"Do ye plan to starve yourself, then?" he asked.

"I'm not hungry," I told him, turning to look back out the window.

"Ye cannot stay up here all day and all night. I am not about to let ye starve yourself to death. If ye wish for the treaty to stand then ye must live, which means ye must eat. I expect to see ye in the great hall for lunch." With that he stormed from the room, slamming the door behind him.

I never left the room, choosing instead to sit and stare blankly out the window until long after the sun had gone down.

Late that night I heard that shuffling outside my chamber again, but this time it was followed by a scratching at my door. Trying to ignore it, I pulled the blankets up around my shoulders and rolled over in bed. A few moments later the sound of scratching came again.

Sighing in annoyance, I climbed out of bed and opened the chamber door. The large black wolf sat before me with a plate of food piled high before it.

"I supposed I'm expected to eat that, am I?" I asked the wolf, crossing my arms over my chest. "Well, I'll tell you the same thing I told your master. I'm not hungry."

I moved to close the door in the wolf's face but stopped when it let out a low, menacing growl. Narrowing my eyes, I glared at it, then bent down and picked up the plate.

"Do you trust me to eat it, or would you like to watch me do that as well?"

The wolf stood up and I jumped back as it padded into the room and dropped itself down in front of the fire.

"Of course," I sighed.

I curled up on the bed, picking over the chicken and vegetables and eating slowly as the wolf watched my every move. My stomach rolled and protested my slow movements, crying out in hunger. If the wolf hadn't been there to watch me, there was no doubt that I would have cleared the plate already. But I did not want it or the MacGregor to know just how hungry I really was.

Seemingly satisfied once my plate was half empty, the wolf turned its back on me and closed its eyes, clearly enjoying the warmth of the flames.

"You know, you're not nearly as fearsome as I once thought," I told it.

The wolf turned to face me and let out a low growl, but upon hearing it I realized that I was no longer afraid. I tore off a piece of chicken, crossed the room to the wolf and stood before it, holding the chicken out in front of me. After a moment it sat back on its hind legs and I tossed the morsel of meat to it. The beast snapped it out of the air deftly, then cocked its head to the side, waiting.

Smiling, I went back to the plate for another piece of meat, this time tossing it across the room and laughing when the wolf moved quickly and caught that piece as well before dropping back down to curl up on the floor.

"We had dogs at the castle," I told the wolf as I sat down on the corner of the bed. "I used to sneak them bits of my supper when no one was looking. My father would warn me off about spoiling them, but I never listened."

A tear rolled down my cheek and I brushed it roughly away, determined not to cry. The wolf stood up and came over to me, and dropped its large head in my lap. I stared down at it, then very slowly raised my hand and placed it gently on the top of its head. When it didn't move I curled my fingers and started scratching slowly, over its neck and behind its ears.

"I miss Fin, my brother. I'll miss riding horses with him. We used to race," I whispered.

I sat in silence for a few minutes, scratching the wolf's ears and enjoying the fact that with it there I did not feel so utterly and completely alone.

After moving what was left of the plate of food to the table I curled up in bed and went to sleep while the wolf watched me from its place in front of the fire.

When I woke up the next morning my room was empty. I finished off my supper from the night before, allowing myself another day's respite from having to face eating a meal in the great hall. But a few hours later the door to my chamber crashed open and the MacGregor stormed in.

"Ye did not come down for breakfast or lunch today, lass."

"I did not feel like coming down to eat."

He glanced over at my dressing table and saw the empty plate there. "Still not hungry, then?"

I blushed and averted my gaze. "Thank you," I mumbled.

"Ye cannot hide up here forever."

"Why not? It's as good a place as any for me to live out my sentence. If I am to be a captive, why can I not be a captive in peace?"

"Is that what ye want? To be locked away with no small sense of freedom?" he asked.

"What I want is to go home!" I shouted. "But since that is not possible, then all I ask is to be left alone. What more could you possibly want from me?" I turned my back on him sharply and dropped my head, wrapping my arms around myself.

A moment later I heard my chamber door close with a slam.

***

That night I heard the familiar scratching at my door and I opened it without hesitation.

"I shouldn't be so glad for your company, knowing that you're here at his behest," I told the wolf.

The wolf nudged the plate of food toward me with its great paw and I picked it up and opened the door wide for it to come inside. It watched me while I ate, eating the morsels of chicken that I shared with it.

The moment I was done eating the wolf padded

over and placed one of its large paws on the door of my wardrobe.

"What is it?"

It padded over to me and nudged at me with its great head until I stood up and walked over to the wardrobe, where it placed a paw on the door again.

I opened the wardrobe door and looked inside, confused. "I don't know what you want. There's naught but clothing in here."

The wolf pawed at my gowns then looked at me. If I hadn't known better I would have sworn it wore an expression of annoyance.

I reached into the wardrobe and pulled out one of the elegant gowns the MacGregor had brought for me to wear and held it up in front of my body. The wolf lifted one of its front legs and brought it across its muzzle covering its eyes, then put a paw back in the wardrobe.

I put the elegant gown back and pulled out a simple blue one instead and held it up in front of me. The wolf dropped back onto its hind legs, looking up at me.

"You want me to wear this one, then?"

The wolf didn't move, just sat there panting, so I took that for a yes. I grabbed the hem of my shift, pulled it over my head, and redressed myself in the gown. Reaching into my closet, I pulled out the simple boots that I had arrived in and pulled them on.

Once I was dressed, the wolf padded over to the

door of my chamber. I opened the door and let it out, but did not step over the threshold myself.

Circling back, the wolf butted its head against my legs, then padded off down the hall again. I looked around but there was no one there to stop me, so I quietly closed the door and hurried down the hall after the wolf.

It led me through the castle and down to the front door, where two men stood guard. I skidded to a stop, staring at them in horror.

"I... I don't..." I stuttered.

"Have a nice night, lass," one of the guards said to me, smiling, then he opened the door for the wolf and me to pass through.

"Thank you," I said quickly with my head down, and rushed out the door, but I came to an abrupt stop when saw the wolf standing next to a saddled horse.

I looked at the horse and then back to the castle. I had mentioned riding to the wolf the night before, and then earlier the MacGregor had asked me if I did not want even a small bit of freedom. Was this his way of showing me that I was not completely captive?

I pulled myself up into the saddle and the wolf took off across the grounds. Pressing my heels into the horse's flank, I urged it forward and then into a full gallop as I followed the wolf across the lush grass of the valley.

The wolf led me to a small lake where it ran headlong into the water. Laughing as I watched it splash around, I climbed down from the horse and stripped out of my gown before diving naked into the water.

I swam out as far as I dared, then rolled over onto my back to stare up at the stars, floating peacefully as the wolf paddled along beside me. It was the first moment since my uncle had tricked me from my bed that I had felt completely at peace.

After a while I swam back to the shore and dropped down onto the bank exhausted. Joining me, the wolf shook its large body, throwing large droplets of freezing cold water over me, and I shrieked when they hit my skin then laughed as the wolf dropped down onto the grass right next to me.

"Thank you," I whispered.

I awoke in the early morning to shuffling in my room to see the wolf's tail disappearing out my door. Rubbing my eyes, I sat up in bed, then hurried out after the wolf. I had been growing increasingly eager to know where the great beast disappeared to every day.

I stuck my head out into the hall to see its tail disappearing into a room a few doors down. I hurried quietly down the hall until I reached the door and pressed my ear to it, listening for a sound, before quietly pushing it partially open.

As I watched, the muscles of the wolf began to roll and shift and my eyes widened as it began to take on the form of a man. I gasped loudly, unable to move as the MacGregor swung around to face me, looking just as horrified as I was.

"Glenna..."

I turned to run but his arm snaked around me like an iron band and hauled me off the floor, pulling me back into his chamber. I opened my mouth to scream but his other hand came up to cover my mouth. My nose was assaulted with the smell of rich, damp grass. Grass that we had been lying in just hours before. When he was a wolf.

I struggled against him and tried to cry out, but he pressed my back against the chamber door, blocking me in with the bulk of his own body.

"I can explain, lass. Please, let me explain." His eyes searched mine, and he kept his hand pressed firmly against my mouth.

I squeezed my eyes shut, sure that this was some sort of terrible dream, but when I opened them again he was still there. I nodded my head slowly and stopped struggling.

"Now if I remove my hand, do ye promise not to scream?"

I didn't move for a moment, then nodded my head slowly again.

The MacGregor removed his hand from across my mouth but did not remove his large body from mine. As the shock of what I had seen slowly started to fade, I became more aware of the fact that his large, naked body was pressed up against me and I flushed warmly. I had not been this close to him since the ride to the castle, but that was nothing compared to this. I could feel every hard inch of him molded against me, and I shut my eyes to force back the wave of desire that was building within me.

"I want to release ye, lass, but I need to know that you're not going to try to run the moment I do. I don't want to have to restrain ye."

"I won't run," I promised, opening my eyes again.

He eased his body away from mine and took a step back from me. I blushed furiously as the entirety of his nakedness came into view. My eyes ran over his body, taking in the broad expanse of his chest and the firm muscles of his stomach, but when my sight dropped down to his manhood I jerked my head up again then turned my face away from him while he covered himself with a shirt and reached for his plaid.

"Ye can look now, lass," he said to me once he was fully dressed in his kilt.

As I waited for him to clothe himself my desire had given way to anger, and I wasted no time unleashing it on him.

"You are a liar and a deceiver, Alastair MacGregor!" I shouted at him. "I fed you from my plate. I swam with you naked. I scratched your flea-ridden belly!"

I looked around the room for something to throw. Snatching a bowl off the side table, I heaved it at his head. The MacGregor ducked and the bowl shattered on the wall behind him.

"How could you do such a thing?" I demanded.

I looked around for something else to throw and picked up a cup.

The MacGregor crossed the room to me in three long strides and grabbed hold of my wrist before I could throw the cup at his head as well.

"Ye were going to make yourself sick. It was the only way I could think of to get ye to eat something. And then ye seemed happy to have a friend in the castle. Someone that ye could confide in instead of spending your days all alone."

"And now you've stolen my secrets. You know things that I would never have chosen to tell you. Ever! And in doing so you've taken my only friend from me, and now I have no one in this wretched place. No one!" I cried as I tried to tug my wrist free.

The MacGregor kept his firm grip on me, but raised his other hand and ran it along my cheek, wiping away the tears that I hadn't even realized had started to fall.

I jerked my head away from his touch. I could already feel my anger ebbing with him being so near to me. But I wanted to be angry. I wanted to keep throwing things until I had broken every single item in his bedchamber.

"I'm sorry for that, lass, I truly am. Ye were not meant to find out this way."

The strength to fight went out of me and I dropped

my head, the tears now running freely down my face. All of the fear and loneliness I had been battling back surged up and overtook me and my shoulders shook as I sobbed.

The MacGregor released my wrist and wrapped his large arms around me, pulling me in to his hard chest. Then he lifted me and carried me over to the bed where he held me on his lap while I emptied myself of my tears.

A long while later the tears had finally stopped but I stayed curled against his chest while he held me.

"What are you?" I hiccupped into his shirt.

"That's going to take a bit of explaining."

"I have time. It's not as if I'm going anywhere."

"Come on, then. Let's get ye a bit of fresh air and I'll see if I can explain."

CHAPTER 8

"My clan has been cursed with the wolf for as far back as anyone can remember. There is no time we know of when it has not been a part of my people," Alastair told me as we strolled through the trees.

After the kindness he had shown me I had started to think of him by his given name instead of as the MacGregor. It was hard not to think of our connection more intimately after all that I had shared with the wolf.

"There are two ways to become a wolf," he continued. "Inheriting it through the blood at birth, or through the bite of a wolf."

"Does that mean every member of your clan is a wolf?"

"No. It does not surface in every child born, only a

select few. Mostly when both parents are wolves, especially if they are both blooded wolves. Like recognizes
like, ye see, and over time we have found other wolves,
not of our clan. When those wolves wed and mated,
they had wolf children. It does not happen as often
when a blooded wolf takes a non-wolf to wife. And I
have yet to hear of a wolf being born to a bitten wolf
and a non-wolf."

I nodded, my mind racing as I scrambled to understand it all. "All of the legends about you, the tales?" I
asked.

"The first tales were started by our own clan long
ago. They believed the only way to keep us safe and to
keep from becoming the hunted was for the MacGregors to position themselves as the hunters."

"So you ensured that the rest of us would be too
fearful of you to ever try to claim your land."

He nodded and continued to walk in silence.

"But how can you stand it? How can you stand
knowing that your named is whispered in fear all
throughout the highlands? That you're believed to be a
rapist of women and an enslaver of children? That you
may be the very devil himself?"

His shoulders went stiff and his hands bunched into
tight fists at his sides.

"I stand it because I must," he said coolly. "I stand it
because I must protect my clan. What the rest of them
out there think of me means nothing so long as my

clan has no need to fear being hunted for what they are."

My heart ached at the pain and determination in his voice and I reached out, laying my hand against his arm. He stood very still for a moment, then covered my hand with his own.

"I'm sorry, lass. I'm sorry that your uncle betrayed ye the way he did in an attempt to appease me. And I'm sorry that you're trapped here now, all for the sake of honoring a bargain that you wanted no part of in the first place."

"Can I not go home, then?" I asked sadly. "Even now?"

He shook his head and removed my hand from his arm. "I'm sorry, lass, but no. There is no way for me to be able to return ye to your father now. I could not explain my actions and maintain my position of power if I did. It would be seen as weak, or as a declaration of war, to hand back what was given to me as a peace offering. This is your home now. There is no going back."

"Is my father to never know what happened to me? My brother? Is my uncle to just get away with whatever poisonous lies he is sure to have spread?" I stood there shaking in fury at the injustice of it all.

"We could write to him if ye like, to let him know that you're safe," he offered.

"Safe?" I snorted. "My father would never for a

moment believe that I am safe knowing that I am here with you. But it would be better he know where I am and about my uncle's hand in all of it than to have to sit and wonder for the rest of his days."

"I'll send a messenger to him, Glenna. I promise you that."

CHAPTER 9

That night I sat at my dressing table and fixed my hair, plaiting it around one side of my head and letting the rest fall loose over my shoulder. After some consideration, I chose a pale green gown to wear with matching slippers. Once I felt sufficiently ready, I took a deep breath and exited my chamber to make my way down to the great hall in time for supper.

I followed the sound of voices until I came upon the great arched room, filled with rows upon rows of tables seating the castle's many inhabitants. Hovering in one of the archways I bit my bottom lip, hesitant to go any farther. I could see Alastair seated at the head table and, as if able to sense my presence, he looked up at that very moment, his eyes focused in my direction.

Now that he had seen me it was too late to make my retreat, so I gathered my courage and swept forward into the room with my head held high.

I could hear the curious whispers from the tables around me as people turned to watch my procession up to the head table. When I reached the dais Alastair stood, along with the other men at the table with him, the ones to his left each moving down the table a seat in order to make room for me.

"Ye look quite bonny this evening, Miss Gordon," he said to me, helping me into my chair.

"Thank you," I said graciously. I inclined my head to him, sliding easily back into the manners that I had been trained to from birth.

"I'm glad that ye chose to join us."

"It occurred to me that if this is to be my new home, it would behoove me to treat it as such. And I thought... I thought that it would be nice to share my evening meal with my... with you, in a more lively location this evening than on previous ones," I said nervously, my eyes flicking quickly over to him and then down to my plate. But not before I saw a small smile tug at the corner of his mouth.

By the time dinner was finished I was feeling decidedly uncomfortable. Never before had I had so many curious eyes focused on me for so long.

"If you would excuse me, I think it's time for me to retire to my room," I told him as I stood up from my seat.

"I'll show ye back to your chamber, then."

Alastair offered me his arm and I took it, allowing him to escort me out of the hall.

"MacGregor," a soft voice called as we started down the hallway toward the staircase.

I turned around to see a lovely young woman swaying toward us. Her long, fire-red hair was a mass of curls that fell over her shoulders, framing a sweet heart-shaped face. Her moss green eyes sparkled as she looked at him and I felt a tinge of jealousy spike through me.

"Oh, I'm sorry. I dinna realize ye were busy." She tore her gaze away from him to glance my way for a split second before dismissing me, then enveloped him in a warm smile. "I was just wondering if ye will be needing anything." She paused meaningfully and leaned in slightly. "Later."

I could not believe her baldness. I was sure that she was trying to make an assignation with him right there in front of me. Not that I had, nor wanted any claim on the man, but it simply was not the thing to be done in front of a stranger. And a female stranger at that.

"No, Allina, I will not," Alastair told her tersely through gritted teeth. He continued up the stairs with his jaw clenched tightly.

I looked back over my shoulder to see Allina staring at me, her eyes full of fire and her hands clenched into tight fists at her sides.

"I'm sorry about Allina," he said when we reached my door.

"I'm sure it's none of my business."

"The lass is young, and fancies herself a wee bit in love with me."

"Does she have any reason to?" I asked him, and then blushed. "I'm sorry. It's just that she was so bold. As if she had a right to be. But as I said, the matter is none of my concern."

But even as I said it I remembered the way she had looked at me. This was no young lass with a crush. The look had been one of pure hatred. I shivered and wrapped my arms around myself.

"What is it, Glenna?" he asked.

"I just realized how lonely I will be here at night now that I won't have the wolf to keep me company any more. I noticed the collection in your study. Would you mind very much if I were to borrow a few of your books?"

"Ye like to read, then?" He looked at me, surprised.

"Very much. I was my father's only child for a long time, so he wanted to ensure that I had a proper education."

"You're welcome to borrow any book ye wish if it will ease your time here, but you'll find more variety in my library than my study. Shall we go now and find something?"

"I would like that very much. Thank you."

My hands slid over the soft spines of the books in his library but my eyes were blind to the words in front of me. It was much too hard to concentrate when I could feel his eyes focused on my back as I made my way around the room.

"This is quite the collection, MacGregor." I looked over my shoulder to smile at him, trying to relieve some of my tension. The air in the room seemed to get heavy whenever we were quiet for too long, as if the very air around us swelled with anticipation.

He leaned against the mantle of the fireplace watching me, an intense expression on his face as if he were working on a puzzle that he was unable to solve.

"Have ye found anything in here that is to your tastes?" he asked me.

"Oh, yes. I could easily lose myself in here for months on end. You'll have to be very careful or you may never see me again. Your library is even greater than my father's. I can hardly believe it."

"High praise coming from you, lass."

I laughed and turned back around to the bookcase. "Do you have a favorite?" I asked him.

"I do," he said simply.

I turned back to him and raised an eyebrow questioningly. "Are you going to tell me what it is, or am I going to have to guess?"

He smiled slowly and nodded toward the bookcase. "Guess."

I stepped toward him, enjoying the new game. "And if I guess correctly, what will my prize be?"

"What would ye be wanting?"

I tilted my head and studied him. "I'm not sure yet. I'll have to think about it."

Alastair straightened himself and came toward me. His long, graceful strides reminded me so much of the wolf I had known that I took a step back, then another, until I bumped into the bookcase behind me.

He stood too close to me, the toes of his boots almost touching those of my slippers. He raised his hands and rested them on the shelf behind me, effectively caging me in.

That was what came of thinking of him like a friend instead of my captor. I should never have joked with him so freely. I couldn't breathe with him so close.

"Are ye afraid of me, lass?"

I swallowed and shook my head. "No, it's just a bit... unnerving. You are nothing like what I was expecting. I thought you would be... wild... and cruel."

"And now?" His deep voice was low, barely above a whisper.

I looked up into his vivid green eyes and resisted the urge to touch him.

"Now I just think you're wild. But how could you not be, being what you are?"

"Aye, lass, I'm wild."

"And dangerous," I whispered.

"Why do ye say that?" he asked, leaning closer.

"Because when you're near me like this, I cannot think straight. I forget who I am and how I came to be here. I forget my loneliness. I forget everything but how badly..." I shook my head, trying to clear it of the fog. "How badly I want you to touch me."

He lifted a hand to cup my cheek, then trailed his fingers down and around the back of my neck.

"If anyone here is dangerous, lass, it's you. My family may be cursed with the wolf, but you... you have bewitched me. Who are you truly, Glenna? Are you one of the fairy folk come to lead me to my doom? For my days are filled with thoughts of ye. Hidden away in your room. Why else would I go to such lengths to be near ye? To try to make ye happy?"

"I'm no fairy," I told him.

"No? A witch, then, come to test me? For from that first moment I saw ye in the woods and heard ye curse your wretched uncle I was taken with ye. Well, I'll tell ye now, sorceress, that whatever test you bring, I'll face it. And I'll face it gladly knowing I'll have this memory to take with me."

I gasped as his hand tightened around the back of my neck and he pulled me forward. I stood frozen as his head dipped down to mine but made no sound of protest as he moved to kiss me. His lips were soft and firm, and I quickly melted into his touch. I felt like I had been waiting for this moment from the first second I had set eyes on him in the woods. No matter how hard I had fought it at the time, I could admit it to myself now.

His free arm came around my waist, holding me tight to him, his fingers splayed over the base of my spine, pressing me in to him. I raised my hands to his chest, my fingers curled, grasping tightly to the fabric of his shirt.

I opened my mouth, a soft sigh escaping my lips, and he deepened the kiss, pressing me back against the shelf as his tongue dipped eagerly into my mouth. I kissed him back hungrily, my arms snaking up to wrap around his neck, pulling him closer as desire flared within me.

Alastair lifted me off my feet and carried me to the couch, laid me back on the cushions and covered me with his body. My breath caught in my throat as his hand ran up my bodice to cup my breast and my back arched, pressing me harder against his palm.

I pulled my mouth away from his as I gasped for breath, but his lips never left my body. I groaned as they roamed over my jaw and down my throat, leaving my skin burning in their wake as his tongue dipped into the hollow of my collarbone. I craved more even though the last sane part of myself told me that we must stop.

"I can't... I can't breathe," I gasped. "I can't think."

"Then don't think," he growled into my ear before his demanding lips found mine again.

I opened my mouth, eagerly accepting him,

silencing the nagging voice in my mind as our tongues dueled. This was surely the road to ruin but I did not care. If this was what ruin felt like, I would accept it gladly.

Through the fog in my mind I thought I heard a door opening, and was brought fully back to myself by the sound of a loud gasp.

Alastair and I sat up quickly to find Allina staring at us in shock. Her eyes were wide above the hand that covered her mouth, watching as I hurriedly tried to smooth my gown before she turned and fled from the room.

"Oh God in heaven, what are we going to do?" I asked him, clutching his sleeve. "She is bound to tell someone."

"No." Alastair shook his head. "She willna." He turned to me and cupped my cheek. "And even though I hate that we were interrupted, the lass probably did us a favor."

I closed my eyes and turned my face into his palm.

"You're right," I sighed. "We let things get much too out of hand."

He stood and held out his hand to me, helped me to my feet, then kissed me softly. I could sense his barely restrained hunger and I felt for him as the same need echoed inside me.

"I'll walk you back to your chamber."

"No," I said quickly, then laughed, stepping away from him. "I mean, it would probably be best if I went back by myself. One close call is more than enough for one night."

I kissed him on the cheek and walked quickly to the door before I could change my mind.

"Will ye be down for breakfast tomorrow?" he asked before I could disappear around the corner.

I didn't reply. I simply smiled before I walked away.

I couldn't keep from grinning the entire way back to my room, marveling at the strange turn of events.

As I reached my door a shiver went down my spine, accompanied by the strange sensation that I was being watched. I looked back down the hallway in the direction I had just come from, but could see no movements in the shadows. Shivering, I quickly opened my door and hurried inside, shutting it quickly once I was inside.

Once I was alone the feeling was gone and I chided myself for my silliness. It was most likely nothing more than my overactive imagination.

CHAPTER 10

a week had gone by since Allina had walked in on us in the library, and it looked like Alastair had been right after all. There hadn't been so much as a whisper of our indiscretion floating around the castle. I was grateful to Allina for her silence, even though I was sure that she hadn't held her tongue for my benefit.

I looked up at the bright blue sky and smiled. It was a beautiful day outside as I walked around the grounds. One of the grooms smiled and waved at me as he led a horse past me and I lifted my hand in greeting. I had been to the great hall for every meal for the past week and the castle's inhabitants had started to become accustomed to my presence.

Alastair had made the official announcement of my arrival the morning after our interlude in the library. I was to be treated as a special guest of the MacGregor and shown every courtesy. Only those who had been there the first night were aware of how I had actually come to be at the castle. As far as anyone else in the clan was concerned I was simply the daughter of a clan chief come to visit for an unspecified amount of time.

I was sure that everyone had their own thoughts and speculations but it no longer mattered to me. I was welcome now, and Alastair's announcement ensured that I was met with no hostility.

I paused and bit my lip, looking up at the great castle. I had not seen Allina since that night and I wasn't ashamed to say that I was grateful for her absence. I knew that if I were to run into her it would be hard to mask my embarrassment over what she had seen. The one thing that continued to nag at me, though, was the fact that I still didn't know why she had been in Alastair's library at that time. Had she heard us from the hallway and come to investigate?

What did it matter? Speculating about it would do me no good.

I wandered out to the stables and waved to one of the young grooms. "Good morning, Ian. How are you today?"

"Very well, thank you, miss. Were you hoping to ride today?"

"If it wouldn't be too much trouble for you to get a horse saddled for me."

"Not at all, miss. It won't take a moment."

I waited patiently as Ian saddled my horse, a beautiful and spirited chestnut mare. I was eager to ride back to the lake the wolf had taken me to and spend some time by the water.

The ride out to the lake was peaceful. It took me a while to find my way but I was able to locate the clear blue waters before too long.

I was lying on my back with my skirts spread out around me, watching the clouds float by, when I heard a shuffling in the trees behind me followed by a low growl.

I sat up quickly and looked around while the mare continued to nibble at the lush grass. Was I hearing things?

The growl came again, louder this time, and I scrambled to my feet and hurried over to the horse.

"I think that's more than enough nature for one day," I said to myself.

I pulled myself into the saddle as a huge wolf stepped out of the trees and into the clearing. I knew instantly that it was not Alastair. Its coat was a light brown, not his deep black. It stalked toward me, head low to the ground, with its sharp teeth bared menacingly.

"I don't know who you are," I said to it, my voice shaking, "but I know what you are. And I will tell you now that if you attack me, you will find yourself in grave trouble."

The wolf snapped its jaws at me and the horse whinnied, finally recognizing the danger. It only made sense that the horse would not have been afraid of the

wolf at first. All of the horses owned by the MacGregors would have had to be trained to be accustomed to
the wolves so that they did not lose control every time
their masters shifted between their wolf and human
forms.

"Please don't do this," I pleaded to the wolf as my
grip tightened on the reins.

The wolf lunged at me and I screamed, digging my
heels into the horse's flank.

The horse shot forward and crashed through the
trees as we raced back toward the castle. I looked back
over my shoulder to see the wolf following close
behind, snapping at our heels.

"Faster," I cried to the horse. "Please, please go
faster."

A low branch slapped me in the face and I could feel
a sharp stinging just below my eye.

I jerked in my saddle as the wolf caught up with
us and brought the horse down beneath me. My
scream mingled with the horse's as we landed hard
on the forest floor, the weight of the horse crushing
my leg.

When the mare struggled to get back on her feet I
was able to pull my leg free, but cried out at the pain in
my ankle. I must have twisted it when the horse landed
on me.

I pulled myself backwards on my elbows, watching
in horror as the wolf sank its teeth into the horse's
neck, savagely cutting off her cries.

"No!" I screamed as it lunged toward me, throwing my arm across my face.

My body tensed in anticipation of feeling its teeth tear into my flesh, but that never came. Instead I heard a loud thump and a sickening crunch. I looked up to see a second wolf rolling with the first, this one with a glossy black pelt.

The wolves tangled together and rolled, snapping at each other.

"Alastair!" I screamed as the brown wolf closed its jaws around one of the black wolf's front legs.

I looked around frantically, looking for something, anything that I could use as a weapon. Reaching up above me, I grabbed hold of one of the thicker branches and bent it back as far as I could, moving it back and forth until it snapped off in my hand, the broken end sharp and jagged.

I ran toward the fighting wolves as they battled for the upper hand. When I got closer I could see a streak of blood through Alastair's black fur and a blinding rage flared within me. Before I could think I ran toward the giant beasts, the thick branch held high in my hands, and I plunged the sharp end of the stick into the brown wolf's side, driving it in as far as it would go.

The wolf howled and turned on me. I stumbled backwards to get out of the way, and as it reached for me it made the fatal mistake of exposing its neck to Alastair. Just like the brown wolf had with the mare, Alastair's giant jaws wrapped around the brown wolf's neck and bit down before he pulled his head away, tearing apart the brown wolf's neck. I whimpered as a warm spray of blood hit my face and coated the front of my dress.

Once the brown wolf lay unmoving in the grass, the wolf I knew to be Alastair limped over to me and collapsed with his large head in my lap, resting a moment before nuzzling my face. I wrapped my arms around his neck and buried my face in his warm coat as my body began to shake.

The wolf stood and started to limp away from me, so I wound my fingers in his fur and followed, wincing internally with every painful-looking step I saw him take.

After a few minutes I understood where he was taking me when I saw the bright splash of red tartan lying across a bush. He must have torn it off and shifted when he heard my cries. I let him go and turned around in order to offer him some privacy as he shifted back into his human form, and I could soon hear the swishing of fabric behind me as he got dressed.

"Glenna, lass." His voice was rough with worry, and I ran limping to him and threw myself into his arms.

One of his arms came around me to hold me tightly as I burst into tears.

"Are ye all right?" he asked me frantically. "Are ye injured? Did it bite ye?"

I shook my head no and continued to sob. I couldn't seem to stop. Whatever clarity had been driving me was now gone and in its absence it had left me a weak, shaken mess.

"I'm sorry," I gasped. "I'm sorry. I will be all right in just a moment."

He pressed a kiss to the top of my head and held me close.

"It will be all right now," he promised me. "You're safe now, lass. You're safe now. He can never hurt ye again."

My shoulders shook harder as I clutched at him, my mind trying to make sense of the close call I had just escaped.

"Come now," he said softly. "We must head back to the castle."

"Oh, Alastair, your arm!" I looked down at the angry-looking wound. Blood dripped from where the skin was torn open. "We must get you help."

"Donnae fash yourself about it. Come, now."

When we got back to the castle, the men gaped and the women hid their faces in horror at my appearance. I could not blame them as I passed by, soaked in fresh blood. I must have looked like some demon creature out of their darkest nightmares come to carry them away.

Alastair's men descended on us as the word spread, but he waved them away.

"I will be with you after I see to Miss Gordon," he told them, hurrying me through the halls and up to my bedchamber.

"You," he said to one of the castle maids as we passed. "Fetch us enough hot water to fill a bath, and be quick abut it."

"Right away, sir," she said quickly before running off.

My bedchamber seemed eerily quiet after the commotion downstairs. My fingers shook as I tugged at my dress, trying to remove it.

"Glenna, wait," said Alastair, grabbing at my hands.

"No." I shook my head. "Get it off me. I have to get it off me. There's so much blood. Please."

Nodding, the MacGregor released my hands and helped me out of my dress, averting his eyes as I stood before him in my thin shift.

"There is a dressing gown in the wardrobe," I told him.

He brought it back to me and held it open for me to slide into, then gathered me up and set me down on the bed.

"Are ye sure you're not hurt?" he asked me again, his eyes darting back and forth as he examined me.

"I'm sure. I was not bit. Just a twisted ankle."

"We'll get it seen to."

"We need to get your arm seen to," I told him. "It will have to be stitched up."

He opened his mouth to say something, but a knock at the door cut him off.

When he opened the door four maids walked in, each holding a very large bucket of water in each hand.

They kept their eyes down as they filled the large washbasin up with warm water.

"I've sent for Mrs. Fletcher to see to your arm, sir," said one of the maids. "She said that she would see to ye in your chambers shortly. Would you like me to stay here and help Miss Gordon?"

Alastair shook his head silently and the girl left.

Taking my hand, he led me to the tub that was separated from the rest of the room by a painted screen. He stood on one side of the screen while I slipped out of my clothes on the other. I sank slowly into the warm water, sighing as it chased away the chill that had settled within me. Taking the washcloth, I went to work scrubbing the blood away from my skin. It had long since dried and caked onto my face and came away in flecks. I watched as my bath water slowly became tinged with a faint red. When I thought of how much blood had soaked my dress I knew that there would be no saving it. Not that I would have been able to wear it ever again even if it could be saved. I never wanted to see it again.

I unplaited my hair and dragged my fingers through it, making sure to scrub every last trace of the wolf's blood from my locks. By the time I was sure all the blood was gone, the water was starting to cool, so I stepped out of it and wrapped the large bath sheet the maids had left around my body.

"I'm coming around," I told him.

I came out from behind the screen and chose a fresh

shift from the wardrobe while he kept his eyes discreetly averted, then crawled into bed.

"Would ye like me to stay with ye?" he asked once I was finally settled.

"No, but thank you. I feel much better now that I've had my bath and all the blood is gone. You should go get your arm seen to."

"But if ye need me..."

"I will come find you."

"I will find out who did this to ye and why, lass. I promise ye that."

"I know you will."

He crossed the room to me and pressed a fierce kiss to my lips. "Try to get some sleep now," he said, brushing back my damp hair. "I'll look in on ye later."

Once he had left I fell back against the pillows and stared up at the ceiling. Would it never end? Was I doomed to spend the rest of my life in this castle, constantly trapped in this room, living under the threat of drowning in my own tears?

I rolled over in bed and slowly opened my eyes to find the chair next to the bed occupied.

"I'm sorry, lass, did I wake ye?" Alastair asked.

"No, it was simply time for me to wake," I told him, reaching out my hand to him. He took it and raised it to his lips and pressed a kiss to my palm. "Have you been here long?"

"I dinna know. It was like time stopped when I entered your chamber. I sat down to watch over ye for a short while, but I'm not sure how long I've actually been sitting here for."

My heart swelled at his words and I squeezed his hand tightly.

"How is your arm?" I asked. His left forearm was wrapped tightly in a white bandage. I was glad that he had gotten it properly seen to. "Does it hurt?"

"Not at all now. It will be little more than a scratch by morning."

I snorted lightly but said no more about it. I knew that it would do me no good. Men were constantly downplaying the severity of their injuries.

"And what of the wolf that attacked me? Were you able to discover anything about it?"

Alastair shifted uncomfortably and averted his eyes. "That's not something ye need to worry yourself about just yet. Why don't ye lie back and rest some more?"

I sat up and narrowed my eyes at him, sure that there was something he wasn't telling me. But I would not be coddled. I had already had enough of that for one day. Now that the shock had passed, I wanted the facts.

"I have rested quite enough. Now, what are you not telling me? Don't you think I deserve to know who it was that would have taken my life?"

His jaw clenched and he sighed, giving in. "All right, then. We discovered that it was a man from the village. He had fallen on hard times over the last few months and he had turned to drink..." He trailed off.

"What is it?" I prodded. "What else did you find?"

"When we searched the man's home we came across some money. Enough money to give us all pause."

I struggled for breath as the importance of his words hit me. "You don't think that someone paid the man to have me killed, do you?" I asked him.

"Glenna, speculating about this will not do ye any good."

"Oh, God," I gasped. "You do think that he was paid to kill me, don't you?"

"I admit that's how it looks," he said with a nod, then hastened to add, "but it makes no sense, lass. Who here would have any cause to dislike ye, let alone hate ye so much that they would do something so evil? It's much more likely that he stole the money and the drink rotted his brain."

Even as I nodded at his explanation, my mind continued to race. There was one person who could hate me that much. After what Allina had witnessed in the library, would she actually go so far? But Alastair had said himself that the girl believed herself to be in love with him. And what was love if not the ultimate form of madness? How far would a madwoman go to remove what she believed to be the obstacle that stood between her and the man she loved? I shivered at the thought.

"Are ye cold?" Alastair asked me.

"Yes, so very cold." I pulled my hand from his and slid over in the large bed. "Will you hold me for a little while?"

He hesitated for only a moment before joining me, and I snuggled in to his side with his large arms wrapped around me.

Sitting up slightly, I pressed a kiss to his lips. "You saved my life today, and I never thanked you."

"Oh, God, Glenna." He crushed me to him and captured my mouth with his, pouring his frustration into the embrace. "When I heard ye scream I thought my heart had been torn in two. And seeing ye there, with that wolf upon ye, I had never been so afraid in my whole life."

I wrapped my arms around his neck and kissed him as hard as I could, pulling him down on top of me as his hands grabbed at my sides, cupping my breasts and caressing my waist.

"I thought I was going to lose ye," he panted into my ear. "I thought I was going to be too late and that I would lose ye."

"When I saw you fighting that other wolf I was so scared that I was going to lose you too that I had to do something," I told him, remembering my fear when the other wolf had bitten Alastair's leg.

Alastair propped himself up on his elbows and looked down at me with wonder in his eyes.

"Ye were so brave, and ye looked so fierce. I was so mad at ye for putting yourself in danger like that by stabbing him, but so proud of ye as well. My little warrior."

I kissed him gently and looked into his eyes. "I couldn't let anything happen to you."

"You're safe now, and neither of us will be going anywhere for a long while," he told me.

I sighed contentedly as his hands slowly continued their previous exploration of my body. I closed my eyes, savoring the feel of his touch. He pulled my shift from my shoulders, lowered it and exposed my breasts to his touch. I gasped when his fingers grazed over the tip of one of my sensitive nipples, then pinched it gently.

His head dipped lower and his warm mouth replaced his fingers, his clever tongue flicking back and forth across the peak.

"My God," I gasped.

He chuckled and continued for a few moments more before kissing his way across to my other breast, ready to give it the same treatment.

Sitting up, he knelt with a knee on either side of my hips, then he grabbed me and roughly flipped me over onto my stomach before coming down on top of me again. This time he kissed a hot trail across my shoulders, pulling my shift lower as he went so that he could continue down my spine.

Even as the direction of his kisses along my back lowered I could feel his hand running higher up my thigh as he tugged the bottom of my shift higher.

With one hand beneath me grasping my breast, he yanked me into a kneeling position, my now bare back flush with his chest, and my shift gathered around my waist like a belt.

I closed my eyes and let my head fall back onto his shoulder as his hand caressed my stomach, slowly inching its way lower until his fingers dipped into the soft curls of my sex.

"Spread your legs for me, Glenna, love," he whispered in my ear.

I felt myself flush at his request but did as he asked, eager for more.

His fingers slid gently along my folds, finding the dampness there, and I squirmed beneath the new sensation. He continued to kiss my neck and shoulders as his fingers found the sensitive bud and began to stroke it rhythmically. I moaned and tilted my hips into his touch as the burning built inside me.

I cried out when his two of his fingers dipped lower and entered me. He slid them in and out of me in the same slow rhythm he had been using and I spread my legs wider to give him better access. My hand dropped down to cover his and keep it in place as he continued to plunge into me and my hips moved involuntarily in time with the pace he set.

"Let go for me, love," he growled in my ear. "Take your pleasure."

"I don't... I can't think," I said, breathless.

His hand began to move faster and with more force inside of me and I clutched at him as my body began to shake.

"Alastair?" I cried out in confusion.

"I know, love, I know. Let go."

"Alastair!" I screamed as the pleasure tore through me, shaking my world apart.

I felt him bite down hard on my shoulder as I rode the wave of my pleasure before collapsing against him, spent.

He cradled me gently and lay us down with his body curled tightly around mine from behind.

"Sleep now, lass," he said, pressing a kiss to my hair.

Sighing contentedly, I closed my eyes and curled in to him, falling sleep almost instantly.

CHAPTER 11

I lay on the couch in the library reading with my feet tucked up beneath me. The last three days had passed in a blissful haze. Even though Alastair had requested I stay inside the castle for the time being, a request that betrayed his belief that my attack was a random one, I did not feel the slightest bit cooped up.

I had spent my days immersed in the great stories the library held and my nights wrapped in Alastair's arms. It was enough to ruin me completely if anyone were to find out, even though I was still technically a maid, but I could not find it within me to care. I loved him.

The door to the library opened and Alastair walked in. A piece of paper was clenched tightly in his fist and worry creased his brow.

"Alastair?" I asked, worried. I sat up and closed the book, then set it beside me. "What is it?"

"I just received your father's reply. I came as quickly as I could."

"Why do you look so troubled?"

"Because, Glenna... your father has declared war on clan MacGregor."

I gasped, my hands flying to my mouth. "No, no, this cannot be. It must be some mistake."

"It's no mistake. He is gathering his men to march on us. They are most likely already on their way."

"But why? Why would he do this when he knows I'm unharmed?"

"I suppose he did not believe my letter."

"But war? Why go to such an extreme when he could simply send someone here, or come himself to see it with his own eyes? No, I cannot believe my father would do such a thing."

"Well, he has, and now I have no choice but to meet him in battle," he said angrily.

"No!" I cried, leaping to my feet. "No, Alastair, you cannot."

"I must, Glenna. Word of your father's action has most likely already started to spread through the highlands. Soon the other clans will start to believe that the MacGregors can be challenged. I must put a stop to this."

"Of course, because God forgive anyone who dares challenge the clan MacGregor," I snapped at him.

"Ye of all people know why that must not happen, Glenna. Or have you forgotten so soon?"

"Yes, yes, I know why. But you cannot expect me to stand by while you march out to kill my people. They are my people, Alastair!"

"I have no other choice, Glenna!" he shouted at me.

"Yes, you do!" I shouted back. "You could say no! You could find another way! But instead you would rather stain the highlands with the blood of the people I love. You are a stupid, pigheaded fool, Alastair MacGregor, but I'm an even greater fool for letting myself fall in love with you!"

"Glenna..." he whispered, reaching out to take hold of my arm. I wrenched it from his grasp and shook my head, then fled the room.

I rushed out of the castle, eager to put as much distance between us as possible. There had to be another way, some way to bring this all to a peaceful resolution. I had to get word to my father.

My mind was lost in thought when a large hand came around from behind me and covered my mouth.

"Hello again, sweet niece," came my uncle's voice in my ear.

I struggled against his grip and he shoved me to the ground. I opened my mouth to call for help, but as I took a breath something hard hit me on the back of my head and my eyes fell closed as I slid into blackness.

***

I awoke in a rundown wood hut. From what I could

see, the entire building was made up of one small room, not even the size of my bedchamber back at the castle.

"Oh, good," said a female voice. "You're awake, then."

I tried to sit up from where I lay on the hard floor of the room but found my hands bound.

The owner of the voice knelt down in front of me and I looked up into Allina's sweet face.

"I wanted to dump a bucket of water on ye but your stubborn uncle said no," she pouted.

I shuffled myself into a seated position. The room tilted and I closed my eyes for a moment until I was sure that everything had stopped spinning. The back of my head throbbed where I had been struck but I had to ignore the pain for the time being.

"Why are you doing this?" I asked her. "What do you want from me?"

She lashed out and slapped me across the face with such force that my head snapped to the side.

"Like ye don't know?" she hissed. "I saw ye! Ye know I saw ye. Seducing the man I love in the library, ye little slut. Did ye really think I would just let ye show up and ruin everything that I've worked so hard for? That I would let ye replace me?"

My face burned where she had struck me and I looked at her in anger.

"I did not replace you, Allina. He was never yours," I said angrily.

"Ye lying bitch. He loves me, I know he does. The

MacGregor's just confused right now, that's all. You've done something to bewitch him. I tried to free him from ye. But you're cunning. Much more cunning than I gave ye credit for. I can see that now. That's the only way ye could have survived. Ye should have died. He promised me he would be able to do it."

So she really had paid that man to kill me. I wasn't sure if I felt better or worse now that I knew it to be fact. But at the very least I wouldn't have to spend the rest of my life in doubt, unsure if someone would make another attempt on my life when I least expected it.

The door opened and my uncle walked in. I sneered at him and looked away. Would I never be free of the man? Was he determined to destroy every chance of happiness that I could find?

"And you, Uncle?" I asked him. "What is your part in this? I would have thought you considered yourself well rid of me?"

"And free of ye I was, until this lass here came to our door not long ago. She sought me out, for which I'm grateful. Otherwise Cameron would have discovered my hand in your disappearance."

"The letter that was sent?" I asked.

"Received by me. The one my brother has is a forgery."

"A forgery with enough lies in it to incite a war," I spat. "Why, Uncle? Are you so much of a coward that you would rather send hundreds of our men to their deaths than face the consequences for your under-handed deeds?"

"What I did, I did for our people!" he yelled. "I did what your father could not. If I had been born the elder I would have had the strength to do what needed to be done without the necessity to sneak around like a thief in the night. If you had had the grace to do your duty, to meet your fate with dignity, then none of this would be happening now. None of it. The deaths of those men will be on your head, girl, not mine." Dougal pounded his chest with his fist once for emphasis.

In that moment I wished for nothing more than to be the witch Allina had accused me of being, for if I had had the ability within me to set my uncle aflame with only the strength of my will I would have done it in that instant. He was maddening, and it took all of my strength to hold my tongue. I wanted to curse him to damnation, but it would do me no good.

"So now what, Uncle? What are your plans for me?" I asked instead.

"Kill you, of course," Allina said with glee.

My eyes went wide at that and I looked at my uncle with disbelief. Even after everything he had done, I had to believe that he would draw the line at murdering his own kin.

"You would kill me?" I asked him, disdain dripping from every word.

He looked away from me, refusing to meet my eye. I had never felt overly affectionate toward my uncle. His coolness toward me had never allowed for it. I had always known he considered me to be overindulged and spoiled, but I had never disliked him until he stole me away from my home. My hatred of him had started to subside as I was filled with my happiness with Alastair. But that hatred raged back to life within me now.

"You are pathetic, Uncle," I hissed, "and less than a man. You will meet justice for this, one way or another. I swear it to you."

In a fury, Dougal grabbed his sword and stormed toward me. I held my breath and raised my chin, ready to meet my death, but instead he raised his hand back and brought the hilt down hard against the side of my head, knocking me unconscious.

I groaned, my head throbbing, but the noise was muffled and sounded very far away.

"And here I was hoping you'd do me a favor and die in your sleep," said Allina. "Of course, if you did that I would have been cheated out of the pleasure of killing you myself."

The light in the room was dim but still hurt my sensitive eyes. I blinked a few times while they adjusted themselves.

"Ye were out for two days, you know. We weren't sure if you would ever wake. Your uncle saw it as a sign that we weren't meant to kill ye." She laughed humorlessly and smiled at me. "Your uncle is a fool if he thinks he can deny me this pleasure."

"Where is he?"

"Out taking a piss, most likely. What do I care?" Shrugging, she brought her hands out from behind her back and I saw that she held a wicked-looking knife.

"Please, you don't have to do this."

"Yes I do!" she snapped. "I will be with him. I have a plan, ye see. I'm going to become a wolf. I'm going to get myself bit. Then we can get married and I can have his bairns. I'll love him better than ye ever could, and he'll be able to see that just as soon as you're gone and I'm like him."

"I don't understand..." My head was still groggy from being out for so long.

"Did ye really think he would marry you, you fool? He will never truly love ye. He can never marry any woman who doesn't have the wolf in her. The clan would never allow it, and he knows that. You are nothing more than a pretty distraction to him. I may have no wolf but that doesn't matter to me, because I can change that. And I will, just as soon as I get rid of ye."

She came at me with the knife held high just as the door opened and my uncle walked in.

"Allina, no!" he shouted, diving at her.

He tackled her to the ground and she slashed out widely with the knife. He grabbed her wrist and slammed her hand repeatedly against the floor until her grip loosened and the knife fell from her hand.

"I'll have the eyes from your head!" she screamed at him. They rolled over as they struggled, Allina's hands curling like claws as she tried to scratch his face.

My uncle closed his hands around her throat and turned his head away to try to protect his face while she scratched at him, tightening his grip and choking the life from her.

I watched in horror as she began clutching and clawing at his hands as she gasped for air, her legs kicking wildly. But he did not release her. He squeezed as tightly as he could, his face bright red as he choked the life from her until, finally, her body went limp.

"Oh my God," I whispered, sliding up the wall and inching away.

Dougal looked up from Allina's slack face and stood up slowly.

"Uncle, no." I continued to move slowly away from him.

"I've killed her, Glenna. I can have no witnesses. Ye would tell your father everything. You're determined to destroy me."

I dodged to get around him but he moved quickly into my path. I tried the other way but he cut me off again. Looking down, I saw the knife that Allina had dropped. It had been pushed wide as she struggled for her life. I dove for it and my uncle lunged at me.

He grabbed me by my ankle and pulled me back but

my fingers curled around the hilt of the knife and I kicked back at him as he climbed up my body. I kicked again and he lost his grip on me. I scrambled forward as quickly as I could and got to my feet. Dougal jumped up and came toward me.

"No!" I screamed and stabbed out, burying the knife into his stomach as far as it would go.

His eyes went wide with shock and he looked down at my hand. I let go of the knife and backed away shaking as he fell to his knees. He stared at me, a look of confusion in his eyes, as if he couldn't believe I had actually done it.

I watched as he fell over to the side, his hands wrapped around the knife. Then, as his eyes closed, I turned and fled to the door.

CHAPTER 12

I burst out of the cabin into the early morning sunlight. The hut was surrounded by a low stone wall, and the horses were tied to a post in the yard. I attached the bridle to one, then saddled the other as quickly as possible and swung up into the saddle. Gathering up both sets of reins I scanned the horizon for something, anything, that looked familiar until I spotted the mountain range that pointed the direction to the MacGregor lands.

I set out as fast as I could while keeping control of the second horse. I was sure that I had killed my uncle, but if by some miracle he survived, I did not want to leave him a way to be able to catch up with me before I could make it back to Meggernie Castle. Blessedly, they hadn't taken me very far. I was sure I could thank Allina's eagerness to spill my blood for that.

Once I had ridden for a few hours I released the

second horse, leaving him to be found by some lucky traveler. Pressing my horse on, I gave him his head and pushed him to his limit. There was no time to waste. I had to reach either my father or Alastair before the battle began.

Soon I could hear the clamoring of voices and shouting coming from the other side of the hill before me. I crested the rise and in the valley below stood the two armies of clansmen preparing for battle. I blazed down the hill just as the battle began, the men running headlong toward each other, their swords held high.

"Stop!" I screamed at the top of my lungs. "Stop!"

But it was no use. I was drowned out by their war cries. I watched Alastair lead his men but I could not see my father.

I continued to drive my horse straight toward the rapidly shrinking gap between the two armies and did not stop when his hoofs hit the battlefield but continued to ride out to the center of the field. I pulled hard on the reins, bringing him to an abrupt stop, and the stallion reared back in protest. I turned him in a wide circle, struggling to bring him to a halt as the men continued toward me from both sides.

I looked around frantically for Alastair at the head of his men and upon spotting him screamed his name.

"Alastair! Alastair, you must stop. You must all stop!"

As the men got closer they began to slow, confused by the presence of a woman on the battlefield.

"Glenna?" Alastair hollered when he got close enough to make out my features. "Glenna!"

He ran to my horse but had to step back quickly when it reared up again. Reaching up, he grabbed the horse by the bridle and helped to pull it under control.

The men around us on both sides began to murmur in confusion.

"Miss Glenna? Miss Glenna, is that you?" came a voice from behind me.

I turned to find my father's man Angus shoving his way toward me. I had never been so glad to see my brother's sword master before in my life.

"Angus. Oh, Angus, thank the Lord. You must find my father and bring him to me," I told him.

"Right away, miss."

I turned back to Alastair, who raised his arms up to me. I let him pull me from the saddle only to be crushed in his embrace before my feet had a chance to touch the ground.

"Where have ye been?" he asked, holding me at arm's length and shaking me before pulling me back into a tight hug again. "Ye were gone. Ye were just gone. I thought that there had been another attack. I thought you were dead. I thought that you'd left me. And I'll be honest with ye now, lass. I don't know which thought was breaking my heart more."

I threw my arms around him and kissed him with all the force I could muster, clinging to him as if he were the lone life raft in a raging sea.

"I was angry with you, so angry, but I never meant to leave you. I was taken by force," I explained as I kissed his lips, his cheek, his jaw. "I will never leave you. I love you."

He shouted with laughter and lifted me off the ground, kissing me again.

"Glenna?" My father's frantic voice reached me. "MacGregor, I demand that you take your hands off of my daughter!" he shouted.

"Da!" I said with glee.

Alastair released me and I threw myself into my father's arms. I had missed him fiercely.

"Glenna, my sweet Glenna, are you all right? What have they done to you?"

"I'm all right, Da. I'm safe."

"I'm here now. I'm taking you home."

I pulled away from him and shook my head. For the longest time I had wanted nothing more than to go back home. To see my father and brother again. But I had a new home.

"I'm sorry, but I'm not going back with you," I told him.

"Why not? Has he threatened you, Glenna? Is he forcing you to stay?" My father looked past me to Alastair, glaring at him with the promise of murder in his eyes.

"It's nothing like that. I... I love him," I confessed.

"You what?" he exploded.

"I love him. The MacGregor has been good to me,

Da. He saved my life. We wrote to you, to tell you that I was safe and that all was well, but Dougal betrayed you. The letter you received was a lie."

"Dougal?"

"It was he who kidnapped me. He took me to the MacGregor and offered him a bargain. Only the MacGregor wasn't the type of man that uncle expected him to be." I turned to smile at Alastair. "He's not the man that any of us expected him to be. So I've chosen to go back with him."

"Have you, now?" my father said suspiciously. "And has he offered you marriage, then?"

I froze and dropped my head. "No."

"Then this is unacceptable."

"Gordon." Alastair stepped forward to face my father. He towered over my da, but my father held himself tall, every inch of him a highland chief. "I love your daughter, and I would have her come with me. I will cherish her, sir, I swear it to ye."

"But you will not wed her?"

"Da, stop, please stop. Can you not see that this is what I want? Now is not the time for this. Please. You will both have time to discuss it. But right now is it not more important that you put an end to this war?" I opened my arms wide, to gesture to the men standing on either side of us.

"I would have peace between us, Cameron Gordon," Alastair said, holding out his hand to my father.

My father looked at me and his expression softened. Taking Alastair's outstretched hand, he shook it firmly.

"And I would have peace with you, Alastair MacGregor. But do not think that this discussion is over."

Grim-faced, Alastair nodded once and I felt a sinking feeling in the pit of my stomach.

Alastair and I lay in my bed, wrapped in each other's arms.

"What's on your mind, love? Ye seem troubled," Alastair asked me as his hand ran up and down my spine.

We had spent our entire afternoon simply holding one another, happy to be safe and together again, the threat of war no longer hanging over our heads.

"I was simply thinking of something that Allina said to me when she held me captive," I confessed.

The hand on my back stopped moving and I looked up into his troubled face.

"I don't want you to waste another moment thinking about that wee bitch," he spat. "I would strangle her with my bare hands for what she's done to ye."

I stroked his face and kissed him lightly. "I know you would. But what she said to me... there was some truth in it. She said that you could not marry her, or me, because we do not have the wolf within us. That your clan would never accept it of you. Because any child you have must be a wolf as well."

He said nothing and I dropped my hand with a sigh.

"So it is true, then, is it not? You cannot marry me," I said sadly.

"I'm so sorry, lass. I love ye. I love ye with all that I am. I will not give ye up. They cannot make me. But no, we cannot marry. Not unless I can find some way to change their minds."

"And will you?" I asked. "Will you try to change their minds?"

"I will try, lass. I will fight every day to keep ye by my side. They will all know of my love for ye and that ye are my choice. I will do everything I can to make them see."

He pulled me close and kissed me deeply until my tension and doubts began to melt away and I was filled with nothing but the feel of him.

We would be together, and I had to believe that he would find a way for us to marry before long. Because now that I had found him I would never be able to let him go. My highland wolf.

CHAPTER 13

The rough, worn wood of the raised platform scraped at the soles of my bare feet. I was not bound, but I found that I could not run. My legs felt as though they were trapped in tar and were able to move only by the will of the mob. Standing in the middle of the village square in naught but my shift, I looked out at the angry faces surrounding me. Neither the voices of the shouting humans nor the howls of the giant wolves could be heard as the group surged forward, pressing me back. I was somehow deaf to their cries but I could see the contorted rage on their faces all too clearly as their mouths formed words that I could not make out.

The smell of smoke filled my nose even as the heat of a nearby flame could be felt at my back. They continued to press forward, their eyes filled with hatred, every face so indescribably angry as they called for my death...

〰

I stood in the darkness of my bedchamber and wrapped my shawl tightly around my shoulders. Though the days were getting warmer, the night air still held a refreshing chill that banished the lingering memory of the flames. The window shutters were thrown wide and I closed my eyes and inhaled deeply, enjoying the cool breeze on my face.

I had awakened from my nightmare to find myself alone, with neither the angry mob nor Alastair's sleeping form to be found. He must have left me sometime in the night to go back to his own room. Though I missed the nearness of him, I had to admit to myself that a part of me was glad to be alone. He would only worry over me until he compelled me to tell him what I had dreamt of, and the truth of it would cause him nothing but added stress and heartache.

He knew that although I was happy to stay here with him at the castle in Glen Lyon, there was a sadness that, no matter how hard I tried every day to banish it, had come to settle within me. But the deepest places of my heart knew the truth of my fears whether I voiced them or not. It was the root of these new fears that continued to haunt my dreams at night. It was the fear that his people would never accept me, and that I would be forced to leave this place, and him.

〰

The next morning I rode down to the small village of Fortingall. It was nice to get out of the keep for a while, and visiting my friend Iona was the perfect excuse to put some distance between myself and the castle walls.

I pulled the kettle off the heat and poured the water for our tea. Iona leaned heavily on her cane, moving slowly around her small kitchen, and placed a few sweet cakes on a plate before setting it on the small table between us.

"Oh, Iona, you didn't have to go through such trouble for me," I told the old woman, touched by the kindness of the gesture.

"Nonsense, dear. You're kind to take the time to spend such a beautiful day with an old woman like me. Ye know that I've no one left to spoil. You've become the closest thing that I have to a granddaughter."

I smiled at her, moved by the generosity she showed me, even though she had so little. I had come to be very fond of the widow, and in the short time that we had known each other I had come to think of her as family as well. My own grandparents were dead and gone, and it was nice to have someone older and wiser whom I felt free to go to for guidance. Especially now that I was so far from home.

"I love coming to spend time with you," I told her. "And besides, without these visits to the village, what would there be to keep me out of trouble at the castle?"

"Not finding much for ye to do up there to fill your days?" she asked.

"Sadly, no. Though it pains me to say, I'm not actually very skilled at anything other than riding. But that's not much of a help to anyone, now is it? It's not as if I can go work with the grooms all day."

"No, I can see how ye might be feeling at loose ends." She nodded. "And the rest? How have ye been sleeping since your last visit? You look as though you've had a rough night of it." Iona leaned in to examine my face closely. The corner of her mouth turned down in a disapproving frown at the dark circles I knew to be beneath my eyes, betraying my troubled night's sleep.

Taking a sip of tea, I shrugged my shoulders slightly and avoided her eye.

"Don't worry, it will get easier," she said, nodding with certainty.

"I try to not dwell on it once I'm awake. I know that nothing will make it easier but time. Almost everyone at the keep and in the village has been perfectly nice to me, but I can't help feeling like an outsider. I was hoping that bringing food to those in need in Fortingall would help. That the people would see that I want to be a part of their lives and this clan, but I still feel very much the intruder," I confided in her. "I can feel their resistance to my being here. It has been three months now, and I swear to you I can feel people's eyes traveling to my waistline, waiting to see if I carry the MacGregor's child. What makes it worse is that I know they would never forgive me if I did."

"Can you blame them, child, for being afraid?" she asked gently.

"No." I shook my head." Of course not. They need to know that there will be an heir who carries the wolf within him. And I want that for Alastair—I mean the MacGregor. But I have no wolf, and I cannot give him a wolf son. He says that it makes no difference to him so long as we are together, but how can that be?"

"He loves you, Glenna, and love is a powerful thing. Before I lost my Liam, it felt like our love for one another had the power to move the very mountains themselves. That's probably why it was such a shock to me when he was taken over by the fever. I never believed that a mere sickness would have the power to take him from me. It was too common, too mortal a way for him to die. It sounds to me, child, like the MacGregor has the same kind of faith in your love as my sweet Liam and I had in ours. You must cherish that, Glenna."

"I do," I told her, quickly wiping away a tear. The way she spoke of her late husband always touched my heart. I prayed that Alastair and I would have as many years together as Iona and her husband had.

"Then you must trust in him. He is a strong man, our MacGregor, in heart as well as body. He has protected this clan as his father did before him and he will protect you."

"He must have the support of the people. He doesn't like to talk about it, but I know that he is becoming disheartened by how hard it has been to sway the clan to the prospect of his taking a human wife. I do not want to do anything that will drive him and his people farther apart. I am willing to wait. I want our marriage to be a joyous occasion. I do not want him to have any regrets."

"You're a sweet lass, Glenna, and no matter what resistance the MacGregor may be facing, I'll tell you here and now that he made a fine choice in choosing you."

I reached across the table and took the old woman's soft hand, squeezing it gently.

"Thank you, Iona. It warms my heart to hear you say so, it truly does."

A scream tore through the air, shattering our soft moment, and we both jumped in our seats and looked to the window. A moment later the door to the house banged open and one of Alastair's men stuck his head inside.

"There's been trouble, miss. I have to go check it out. Will you be safe here for a while?" he asked.

"Of course she will," said Iona.

"I'm coming with you," I told him, then put down my teacup and hurried to the door.

"I don't think that's such a good idea, miss," he said as I shoved past him.

"Don't be absurd, Gregory. If there is trouble I'm not about to hide inside. I want to help if I can. Now, which way did the scream come from? We're wasting time."

"This way," he said, apparently deciding that arguing with me on the matter was not a battle worth fighting.

"Thank you, Iona," I said, kissing the old woman quickly on the cheek before I hurried out the door.

Gregory and I rushed toward the town center where a large group of people had gathered and were talking in hushed voices. My step faltered as I flashed back to my nightmare from the night before, but I quickly shook it off.

"Excuse me," I said as I pushed my way through the crowd. "Please let us through. We need to see what's happened."

We broke through the front of the group to see what it was that had drawn everyone's attention, and I gasped at the grisly sight. I turned my face away for a moment while I steadied myself in order to turn back and face the scene.

The body was propped up against the low garden wall. The young man's face was bloated and discolored, and his blank eyes stared right through us.

Gregory looked around at the crowd.

"Who saw what happened here?" he asked. "Did any of you see this happen?" He was met with silence as the people continued to mutter amongst themselves.

"Do any of you know him?" Gregory asked more urgently. I searched the faces for a glimmer of recognition, but no one seemed to know who the dead man was.

Gregory stepped closer to examine the body, looking it over for any signs or marks. There was no blood anywhere that I could see, so I didn't think that he had been stabbed.

"What's this, then?" he mumbled to himself, examining the face more closely. "There looks to be something in his mouth."

"Good Lord in Heaven," came a stunned voice from behind me, and I turned around to see Father James MacGregor crossing himself as he stared wide-eyed at the body.

Standing next to him was the magistrate, making his own half-hearted attempt at the sign of the cross while he blinked slowly, looking for all the world like a very confused, very bloated owl.

"It looks like he's been with our Lord for a while now, Father," said the magistrate.

"Mr. MacAlpin, what would you have us do with the body?" I asked the magistrate as he mopped his brow. His round face was flushed red with exertion from his rush over and his large chest rose up and down as he tried to catch his breath.

"Ah, Miss Gordon, I did not see you there," he said to me, his mouth turning down in a slight frown.

I tried to hide my annoyance. I knew that he had been one of the most vocal at expressing his thoughts about my marrying Alastair, and that he was very much against it. I tried not to let that color my actions toward the man, but it was hard to smile and defer to him when I knew he was set on squashing my happiness. Even if I did understand why.

"It's nice to see you, Mr. MacAlpin," I said to him politely. "But if you would, the body?"

"Of course, of course. A grisly bit of business this. Well, we had best be getting him out of the square." He came forward and turned to face the crowd. "If everyone would please step back and clear a path. Yes, that's right, clear a path, please. And maybe if we could have a few volunteers. Yes, the two of ye." He pointed at two strong-looking young men. "If ye wouldn't mind giving us a hand moving him to my offices? Very good."

Mr.MacAlpin, Father MacGregor, Gregory and I made our way to the magistrate's office with the other two men following closely behind, carrying the body between them.

"There, put him down there," Mr. MacAlpin told them, gesturing to a long, rectangular table in one of his back rooms. "Now, let's examine him and see what we might find."

"There looks to be something in his mouth," said Gregory.

The magistrate looked around the room and grabbed a quill from the sideboard. Coming back over, he handed it to Gregory and urged him toward the body.

Gregory took the quill and used the tip to carefully

fold back the dead man's bottom lip, revealing a large tuft of hair. Taking hold of it gingerly between his thumb and forefinger, he gave it a tug, and pulled a large strip of fur from the man's mouth.

"Good God," I whispered. "Was the poor man strangled with that?" I lifted my hand to my lips, remembering the night just a few months ago when I had a gag shoved into my own mouth. I could still recall the dirty, sweaty taste of it, and the fear. So much fear.

I looked away from the body, overwhelmed, while I took a steadying breath before facing it again.

"This is most certainly murder," I whispered.

"I would say you're right about that, miss," said Gregory.

"Murder, in Fortingall?" blustered Mr. MacAlpin. "But how can that be? We don't have murders in Fortingall."

"Well, you have now, Mr. MacAlpin. And until you find out who did it and why, I doubt that any of us will be feeling very safe in our beds tonight."

"Are you trying to tell me how to do my job Miss Gordon?" the large man bristled. He puffed out his wide chest, and his double chins jiggled as he turned on me.

"Of course not, Mr. MacAlpin," I said soothingly, while internally I rolled my eyes. "I'm simply commenting on the fact that I will feel very relieved once the culprit is caught. I have no doubt that you have the matter well in hand. Why, I'm sure that your clever mind has already begun working on a way to trap the monster that did this."

Mr. MacAlpin grunted, then turned his back on me once more, and I stuck my tongue out at him, giving in to a moment of childishness. There was a soft cough and out of the corner of my eye I could see Gregory trying to smother a smile. I had been caught out. I straightened my face quickly and tried to look as innocent as possible. No matter my dislike of the man; murder was a serious matter and Alastair would need him to dispense justice once the culprit was found. It was no time for me to allow my emotions to get the best of me.

"We should get you out of here, miss," Gregory said to me. "The MacGregor will need to be told about this straight away, and you will be much safer back at the castle. There's not much more we can do here for now."

"Of course," I said to him. "Mr. MacAlpin, Father MacGregor, I hope that you will excuse me if I leave you now. I'm sure that you will be able to conduct your business better without having me underfoot."

"A pleasure to see you again Miss Gordon, even if it was under such unfortunate circumstances," said Father MacGregor with a bow.

"Good afternoon Miss Gordon," said the magistrate gruffly, with the barest incline of his head.

"Good afternoon to you both." I turned and walked out the door as gracefully as possible, trying to not give in to my urge to slam the magistrate's front door.

"What an odious little man," I snapped once Gregory and I were safely outside.

"He doesn't have much love for ye, Miss Glenna, that much is for sure, but I don't know if 'little' is how I would be describing him." Gregory caught my eye and winked and I failed at stifling a giggle.

"Oh, well," I said with a sigh. "There's nothing I can do about it now. I doubt I will ever be able to win the man over."

"I've been coming with ye to Fortingall for the past two months now, watching ye visit the needy and bringing them what you can from the castle. You've a kind and gentle heart. You've taken to our people as if they were your own. And if it means anything to ye, I want ye to know that I would be proud to call ye Lady MacGregor."

"Oh, Gregory, thank you. It does mean something to me, more than I can express." I smiled brightly at him, then headed for where we had left our horses tethered. "Come on. We had best hurry about getting the news of what happened here to the MacGregor."

CHAPTER 14

*T*he air in the forest was crisp and I could see my breath on the air as my small heart beat rapidly with fear. My beautiful mother held a knife high above her head. Her long blonde hair framed an angelic face with crystal blue eyes, now wide and wild with fear.

A low growl came from out of the trees and I whimpered in fright. My mother took a step closer just as I was knocked down by an enormous animal. In the next moment the monstrous wolf was on top of my mother in the snow. With a swipe of its massive paw it tore her throat open and her blood spilled like countless rubies upon the pure white ground.

The wolf looked up from my mother's body and turned to face me.

"Glenna." The wolf's voice was a low rumble from deep within its throat.

"Glenna," came the voice again, this time more insistent...

~

"Glenna. Glenna, wake up, lass."

Large but gentle hands shook me by the shoulders, pulling me from my dream, and I opened my eyes to see a large form leaning over me in the dark bedchamber.

"Alastair?" I asked, my mind still foggy from sleep.

"Ye were having a nightmare. Are ye all right now?"

"I think so. I'm sorry, I didn't mean to wake you. Go back to sleep."

"Do ye want to tell me about it?" he asked, pulling me into his arms.

I curled up against his side and rested my head on his chest, listening contentedly to the steady rhythm of his heartbeat as it pounded soothingly beneath my ear.

"It was nothing, really." It was not like me to hide my feelings from him, but this dream was not something I knew how to share.

"Tell me anyway, love. It's not good to keep these things inside. Maybe it will give ye a bit of peace." His voice was low and thick from interrupted sleep and he ran a firm hand up and down the length of my back, urging me to confide in him.

"It's an old nightmare. It started when I was young. I hadn't had it for quite a few years, but then it started again a few months ago... just before I met you."

"Am I the thing of nightmares, then?" he asked me, only half-joking.

I swatted him playfully on the chest. The fact of the matter was that throughout most of the Scottish highlands the name Alastair MacGregor really was the stuff of nightmare and legends, even if that reputation was mostly unfounded. But none of that mattered to me, because I knew the man he truly was, and the kind and loving heart that beat within his broad chest.

"It had naught to do with you. The dream was about my mother. She died when I was but six years old."

"Ah, lass, I'm sorry for your loss. But why would seeing her again give ye such bad dreams?"

I bit my lip, unsure of how to proceed.

"There is something about my past that I've yet to tell you," I confessed. "It wasn't meant to be a secret. I just couldn't see what difference it would make."

I fell silent again and he nudged me with his leg, encouraging me to continue.

"You're not the first man cursed with the wolf that I've met. At least, I don't believe that you are."

Alastair froze but stayed silent. I could feel his entire body go tense against me.

"I didn't know, Alastair. I swear to you that I didn't know before you explained it to me. My mother and I were out for a walk one day in the trees behind my father's keep. It was deep winter, with a thick layer of snow on the ground. I can't actually remember any of this, mind you. I only know it from my dreams. In them I look down at the snow and my mother is there, lying dead before me. Her empty eyes are staring at me and her throat is torn open. I turn around and a wolf lunges at me. It's the largest creature I've ever seen. It had killed her and now it was going to kill me."

"Oh, Glenna, my love."

"My father said that my childhood mind had turned the man or men who had killed my mother into monsters so I could understand the horror of what I had witnessed. Eventually the dreams faded, but they returned a few weeks before my uncle took me. That night at your camp when I saw the wolf, I finally knew my dreams for truth. That I truly had seen a giant wolf that day. This dream was different, though. My mother was alive and brandishing a long knife aloft. She must have heard the wolf before I did and was trying to protect me."

"Why did ye never tell me?" he asked.

"To what end? Speaking of it would not bring my mother back. And I did not want you to think that I blamed you or your people in some way. Like you said, there are others out there cursed with the wolf, not just the MacGregors. It could have been a Gordon, for all I know."

"I suppose you're right. I just hate to think that ye'd one more reason to fear me before ye knew the truth of who I was," he said.

"But I do know the truth of you, and no dream or

events from my past will change that, or my love for you."

He pulled me up from his chest so that we were face-to-face and kissed me softly until my lips parted for him so that he could slide his tongue past them. I sank into his embrace, running my hands through the light sprinkling of dark hair on his muscular chest.

He rolled me over onto my back and covered my body with his own. Wrapping my arms around his neck, I drew him down to me, enjoying the comforting weight of his much larger body. He kissed me slowly through my shift, over my chest and down into the valley between my breasts. My nipples hardened and I took a sharp intake of breath as the sensitive peaks brushed against the fabric.

With a deep chuckle he took the fabric between his teeth and tugged the front of my shift down, exposing the soft skin of my breast to his wandering mouth. I groaned with pleasure as his clever tongue swirled circles around first one nipple then the other, flicking them as he passed.

I ran my hands up his back and over his broad shoulders, pulling up the back of the shirt he had been sleeping in so that I could press my palms against his warm flesh.

Sitting up, he pulled the shirt over his head and tossed it aside. The shutters were closed and I could only make out the shadowed shape of his naked form on the bed before me, but simply knowing that he was there, completely exposed to me, made my heart beat faster.

I licked my lips as his hand found its way to my ankle, then slid up my calf and along the outside of my thigh. My heart began to race as it continued its journey inward, his fingers tripping across the front of my sex only to dip between my thighs, his thumb probing between my damp folds to find my sensitive bud.

I moaned and let my head fall back as he moved his thumb in small circles, pressing firmly at my core, until the pleasure in me started to build. After a minute the pressure disappeared and I whimpered at the loss. Alastair moved up and positioned himself between my legs and I could soon feel the head of his hard length teasing the entrance of my sex.

"Alastair," I panted, struggling for control of my need. "We cannot. You know we cannot."

He continued to kiss my shoulder but the probing beneath my legs stilled.

"Tell me again why we must not," he said, his voice strained.

"Because I cannot risk getting with child. I am not your wife."

"I love you, Glenna, and I would have you as my wife. We would be married now if the choice were mine alone," he sighed.

"I know," I told him, lifting his head so that I could

look him in the eye in the dark. "But it is not. I am not yet your wife. And I will not risk giving you a son or daughter who does not carry the wolf within them. I will not do that to you, and I cannot do that to your people. You must have their support, and with my being here like this with you, there are many who resent me."

With a heavy sigh he moved off of me and fell back onto the bed.

"I know not how many times I have to tell ye that I would cherish any bairn ye were to bear me."

I smoothed my shift down over my knees and turned to him.

"I know you would. But I also know that a part of you would always regret that they did not have the gift. How would they gain the support of your people to lead? And if it were a son? Could we deny him his claim to be chief, simply because we were unable to temper our passion?"

"Am I to never lie with you as man and wife?" he grumbled.

Even as my heart went out to him, my patience was growing short with his stubbornness and unwillingness to see the truth of my words.

"You may lie with me as my husband when I am your wife, Alastair MacGregor," I snapped. "Or have you already given up all hope that you will be able to sway your clan in our favor? I love you, and would give myself to you completely. But I am not so blinded by my need that I cannot see the truth of our situation for what it is."

"I am the chief. I should be able to marry whomever I choose. With all my power, how is it that I am unable to do this one simple thing?" he asked.

I reached out and caressed his cheek, feeling the light stubble scratch against my palm.

"Because, as with everything else you have done, deep down you know that you must do what is best for your clan, no matter what your heart desires," I said sadly.

"The devil take my clan," he cursed.

"You do not mean that. Be mindful of what you say, lest someone take your words to heart."

Alastair grabbed me by the front of my shift and pulled me roughly against his body. His mouth crashed against mine and I submitted to the fury of his kiss, letting it overtake me. Our tongues tangled as he gathered my hair in one hand and yanked my head back, taking the kiss deeper.

"Ye are mine," he growled into my mouth. "No matter what comes, know that ye are mine."

He released me, stood up from the bed, and gathered his plaid from where it lay on the chair.

"Where are you going?" I asked.

"Back to my chamber. You'll have no peace if I stay here, and I need to think."

My heart sank as he fastened his kilt and walked to the door.

"I will see ye in the morning," he said before slipping out of the room.

Once he had left I dropped back onto the bed and wrapped my arms around one of the pillows, holding it close. The room suddenly seemed incredibly empty with him gone.

CHAPTER 15

There was a flurry of activity in the lower hall the next morning as I made my way through the castle. I hurried toward the sounds of shouting to see three of Alastair's clansmen carrying a fourth, unconscious, man between them.

"What's happened?" I asked them as they lowered the man to the stone floor. "Who is he?"

"We don't know, miss," said one. "We found him on the road like this."

My mind raced as I tried to think of what to do. "Bring him with me," I told them. "He must be seen to."

The man was picked up and brought with me to one of the guest chambers, where I directed them to lay him on the bed.

"Fetch me a bowl of hot water and another of cold. I will also need some fresh cloths. And see if Mrs. Fletcher has any willow bark for when he awakens."

"Right away, miss. Should we bring Mrs. Fletcher to see to him?" one of the men asked.

"No, there is no need. I'm sure she is busy enough already. I'll see to him myself."

The clansman nodded and hurried out the door with the others.

I put my hands on my hips and looked down at the bed, studying the unconscious man before me. His face and clothes were torn and covered with dust and dirt. It had mingled with the blood and sweat on his face, forming thick, cakey patches.

After the men came back with the items I had requested, I wasted no time in carefully cleaning away the blood and grime from the injured man's face.

By the time I was finished, the bowl of hot water was dark brown and the extent of the injuries on his face was exposed for my examination. I could see clearly that he had a black eye and a split lip, with some bruising along his upper cheek, but not much more damage had been done to his face. I bit my lip and wondered about the extent of the injuries to the rest of his body.

I could not strip him. But maybe, if I were to simply lift his shirt to see if there were any major injuries that needed to be seen to?

I moved hesitantly at first but then with more determination. Moving the top part of his plaid aside, I tugged his shirt from his kilt and raised it over his stomach to expose his chest, revealing a smooth expanse of muscle.

I could feel the warmth rising in my cheeks as I examined him, but tried to ignore it as I took in the extent of his injuries. Large patches of bruises covered his chest, as if he had been badly beaten. I prayed that nothing was broken.

First a man had been found murdered in the village, and now another had been beaten and left on the road. There was a violence working its way through Glen Lyon, something ugly and sinister, and I worried that these attacks were only the beginning of the viciousness that we were yet to see.

I brushed the light brown hair back from the man's face with a gentle touch. He would have to be questioned eventually. There was a chance that he would be able to identify his attackers and bring them to justice. Hopefully Alastair was having better luck in the village.

The setting sun bathed the room in a warm orange light as I quietly read and sipped my tea. There had been little movement from the injured man over the last few hours other than some slight shifting in his sleep, but I refused to leave his side on the small chance that he would awaken while I was gone.

The door opened behind me and I turned around to find Alastair standing in the doorway.

"I was told ye were in here," he said as he bent down to kiss me. "Is this our man, then?"

"Yes. He's been asleep all afternoon."

"Why don't ye come away, then, and have some supper with me? Ye should have a bit of rest."

"I've already eaten," I told him, pointing to the empty plate on the side table. "And I'm not that tired, truly. Other than tidying him up, there hasn't been much for me to do. My only worry is that he may have broken a rib or two. There is an awful lot of bruising. I'll not be able to tell for certain until he wakes, though nothing feels like it shouldn't to the touch. But, please, I want to know about your day. Were you able to find anything more out about the man in the village?"

Alastair heaved a sigh and ran his hand through his thick black hair, his emerald green eyes flashing in annoyance.

"Nay, 'tis the same as before. Four days now and hours of questioning, yet not a single person has been able to give something of use."

"But how can it be that no one saw anything the slightest bit suspicious? How could a body just have been placed in the square with no one the wiser?" I asked.

"I wish that I knew, love, truly I do. I'll not sleep easy knowing that a murderer may have slipped through our fingers." His hands clenched into fits at his sides.

"It was very strange, the way he was killed. Why on earth would someone choke him with fur like that?" I asked.

"Glenna, I know you're worried, but I don't think that this is something I should be discussing with ye. It's a grisly business, murder."

"Do you think I speak of this lightly? That I am one to be coddled and protected? I killed my own uncle Alastair. My hands are not free of blood. I can discuss these things without the need to cover my eyes and hide from the truth. I am not so fragile that I will break to think of the uglier things in this world."

He dropped to his haunches and took my hand in his, bringing it to his lips to kiss my fingers.

"You've seen more horror than you've a right to. And I'll not see ye cry over spilling your uncle's blood. Dougal would have killed ye. Ye had no choice. You're a strong woman, my little warrior, of that I've no doubt. But can ye blame me for wanting to protect ye from more pain and suffering when you've already seen so much?" He nodded toward the man on the bed. "And even when I leave to clean up one mess, another finds its way to ye."

"I don't mind getting my hands a bit dirty when the need arises," I told him.

"Aye, and I'm sure they'll get plenty dirty before the end."

"Well, if you won't tell me anything else, for now at

least tell me this. Do you think that this murder is the only one we will see?"

He clenched his jaw, but then shook his head, giving in. "No. I don't think it is."

CHAPTER 16

*E*arly the next morning I stifled a wide yawn and balanced a large cup of willow bark tea on a tray as I quietly let myself into our injured guest's bedchamber. I had left Alastair to attend to the affairs of the day after we had enjoyed breakfast together in the great hall. Until things quieted down a bit, I didn't doubt that we would be seeing much less of each other.

"You're awake," I said in surprise as the door swung open to reveal our injured guest standing with his back to me, looking out the window.

He was wearing the freshly laundered plaid and shirt that I had laid out for him in case of such an occasion. Alastair had stripped the man of his clothing the night before at my behest and settled him properly into bed. It looked as if the long rest had done him some good.

"Are you sure you should be standing?" I asked.

"Probably not," he said with a smile, "but I wanted to stretch my legs a bit. Have ye been the one watching over me, then?"

"Yes. I am Glenna Gordon, and you are at Meggernnie Castle, as a guest of the MacGregor."

He gave me a stiff bow and shuffled over to the chair.

"Thank ye, Miss Gordon, for your hospitality. I am Camden Holme."

"A pleasure to meet you, Mr. Holme, though I wish it were under slightly less painful circumstances. How are you feeling this morning?"

"The truth of it is not fit for a lady's ears, I'm afraid, but I'm sure that under your gentle care I will be feeling much better by the day's end."

I laughed at that and waved him off. Whatever else this man might be, he was a charmer, that was for sure. He had a fast tongue and a smooth way about him. I admired the fact that he could be in such good spirits after his ordeal.

"How is the pain in your ribs?" I asked. "Do you think they may be broken?"

"They're sore for sure, but not broken. I broke a rib once when I was younger. That's not a pain ye soon forget."

"How did it happen?"

He chuckled and shook his head. "I was young, maybe fourteen. My father had a stallion that he was trying to break in. A horse so spirited that I'm sure it was part demon. My father told me that I was to stay away from the beast until he was broken, and of course no young man with any sense of pride wants to be told that something is too dangerous for him."

"Oh, please, tell me you didn't," I gasped.

"Aye, I very much did," he said with a nod. "One afternoon when my father was away and I was to be at my chores, I snuck out to the stables, determined to ride the great brute. It took me longer than I care to admit just to get him saddled. I landed in the dirt more than once. By the time I had him out to the paddock, my resolve was set. I would ride him or die trying."

"It sounds like that was a very likely possibility," I said.

"Aye, it was. I swear, the horse lulled me into a false sense of ease, just so that I could climb up onto his back. The moment I was seated, he bucked wildly and tossed me off, then kicked me squarely in the ribs once I had landed. I barely had the strength to roll away. I was eventually found lying in the grass outside the paddock, while the horse stood by grazing peacefully, as if he hadn't just tried to kill me. My father was furious with me."

"And the injuries you suffer from today," I said, pointing to his face. "I take it they are not from another spirited horse."

The smile fell from his face and he shook his head. "No, they are not."

"Can you tell me what happened to you?"

"I was attacked on the road. The men were not known to me. And though it pains my pride to admit it, they overpowered me, robbed me, and left me for dead."

"Would you know them again to see them?"

"Aye, I think that I could identify them if they were before me."

I walked toward Alastair's study just as the door opened and Mr. MacAlpin walked out. His mouth turned down in a frown upon seeing me and he nodded curtly in my direction.

"Miss Gordon," he said tersely.

"Mr. MacAlpin. I hope that all is well."

"No, Miss Gordon, it is not. But I'm sure that the MacGregor will tell you all about it shortly. Now if you'll excuse me, I must be on my way."

"Have a good day," I told him as he brushed past, bumping into me but not stopping to excuse himself.

I sighed and tried to forget about the encounter. I had enough to worry about without adding the magistrate's rudeness to my pile.

I knocked on the study door then poked my head inside. Alastair was sitting in his chair with his feet up on the desk. His eyes were closed and he was running his hands roughly through his hair, a sure sign that Mr. MacAlpin had brought him bad news.

"May I come in?" I asked quietly.

He opened one eye to look at me, and I saw a bright flash of emerald green before he closed it again.

"Aye, love," he said wearily. "I could use ye if you've got the time."

"What's wrong?" I asked as I closed the door behind me and crossed to the large leather chair opposite his desk. "I just met Mr. MacAlpin in the hall. He was looking even more dour than usual, as amazing as that may seem."

"I cannot blame him for it today, lass. He came here with grave news today."

My stomach clenched at his words. I already knew what he as going to say, though I prayed I was wrong.

"There's been another murder, hasn't there?" I asked quietly.

"Aye, there has. A young woman this time."

"Was it done in the same way? With the fur?"

"Yes, it was the first thing they looked for." His feet dropped from the desk onto the floor and he fixed me with his piercing gaze, frustration in his eyes. "Someone is trying to send us a message, and I'm worried that I already know what it is."

I started at him. "Really? What do you think it is?"

"I don't think there's much chance of it being a coincidence with the fur. I've a feeling that someone may have learned of our secret."

"But how can that be? Your clan has done everything it can to ensure that the secret of your true nature is never revealed."

"Then why the fur, Glenna? What other meaning could it possibly have, if not to taunt us with their knowledge of our curse?"

"If they believe that they know the truth of you and your people, then they take an awful risk with their actions. Why would they risk trying to kill someone who could transform into a giant beast at any moment?"

"I dinna know. But somehow they were able to accomplish the task and kill not one but two of my people. Whoever this person is, they are cunning."

"Alastair, we must find them. We must find them and stop them before they kill again, or the villagers will start to panic. They may even turn on each other in their fear."

"Aye, lass. We won't stop searching for those who did this. And when I find them, they will see justice at the end of my sword."

I stood and walked around the desk to take his face in my hands.

"I know that you will put a stop to this," I told him, placing a soft kiss on his lips.

He wrapped his arms around my waist and pulled me down onto his lap.

"Kiss me again for luck," he said, and his hand wrapped around the back of my neck and pulled me close.

I wound my arms around his neck, and my breasts pressed against his hard chest as his lips met mine for the second time. I sighed as our kissed deepened and let our problems fall away, taking a moment to simply enjoy the nearness of him.

Our embrace was interrupted by a knock on the study door and I hurried to remove myself from Alastair's lap. While all of the castle occupants knew of our love for each other, it would do us no good to be found in such a compromising position.

"And where do you think you're off to so quickly?" he asked as he made a grab for me to tug me back down onto his lap.

"You're needed," I said, swatting at his hand as I sidestepped out of his reach.

There was another knock at the door, this time more insistent.

"I'm not here!" Alastair shouted through the door to whomever was on the other side.

He stood up from his chair and came toward me with determination in his eyes, but I rushed for the study door before he could get his hands on me again.

"Away with you," I yelped. "You've work to do and no good will come of you trying to put it off."

I reached back and groped blindly for the door handle, finding it just as a knock came for the third time. Standing up on my toes, I grabbed Alastair by the shirt and pulled his face down to meet mine, giving him a hard, swift kiss.

"I'll see you soon," I told him, then pulled the door open.

A thoroughly disgruntled older man stood on the other side of the door. He raised his eyebrows upon seeing me and struggled to conceal the smile that was tugging at the corners of his mouth behind a dour scowl.

"Hello, Donald," I said with a laugh.

"Well, then, now I know why I've been all but ignored," said Donald.

I could feel Alastair still hovering behind me, and I looked up to see him glaring at Donald.

"If you're feeling neglected, old man," Alastair said, "then feel free to go somewhere else. I'd hate for ye to stay where ye dinna feel welcome."

"Chief or no, there are times my hand itches for the days when I could take it to your backside," Donald told him.

"I dinna doubt that for a second, Uncle," Alastair said with a wink. "Good thing I've grown too big for such treatment, aye? For I doubt my being chief alone would be enough to deter ye for long."

Donald grunted and I stepped aside so that he could enter the room.

"I'll see the both of you a bit later," I told them.

"Aye, love, have a good afternoon," said Alastair.

"I had meant to tell ye that ye look quite bonny today, lass," said Donald.

I took Donald's hand in mine and gave him a quick

kiss on the cheek. He had been the first of the MacGregor clansmen to show me kindness on the night my Uncle Dougal had traded me to Alastair in exchange for a promise of peace, and I had come to grow even more fond of the older man during my time with them.

"Thank you, Donald. That's very sweet of you to say."

The older man flushed bright red and cleared his throat, waving away my thanks. With a smile to Alastair I slipped out the door, leaving them to discuss their business in peace.

CHAPTER 17

"*A*re you sure you're quite ready for this, Mr. Holme?" I asked for the third time as our horses walked along slowly side by side, away from the castle. I knew that I was being overly cautious, but I couldn't help but watch his expression for any sign of pain or discomfort.

"Aye, Glenna, dinna fash yourself. I'm feeling stronger than I look, I promise ye that," he reassured me.

It was a beautiful summer day, and after a week of forced bed rest, Mr. Holme had been quite insistent about his need to get out of the castle for a bit of fresh air. My suggestion of a short walk around just outside the keep had been thoroughly and emphatically dashed, with him preferring to go for a ride instead.

I couldn't help but feel like his request was dubious

at best. While the bruising on his face and ribs were fading, they still looked painfully sore. From the first day Mr. Holme had been brought to the castle I had felt responsible for him, and I didn't want to do anything that would slow the progress of his healing.

I had given his description of the attack and his assailants to Alastair, who had then added it to his ever-growing collection of clan responsibilities. Alastair had confided in me that the chances of finding the men who had done this were very slim, as they could have moved out of the area immediately.

With everything that had been going on, I was furious about the lack of justice I was seeing. Was everyone to get away with their unspeakable crimes, sneaking off like cowards under the cover of night? In the past few months I had seen more ugliness in the world that I ever had in my entire life. I had never considered myself overly sheltered or protected from the realities of life. But these days, my life before my uncle Dougal had betrayed me seemed to be a long stretch of sweetness and ignorance.

At least my uncle had paid for his crimes in the end. Even if it had been with his life.

Mr. Holme and I rode until we reached a wide, clear expanse of the glen.

"This is a beautiful area," he remarked, looking out over the gently sloping hills.

"The Gordon lands have always filled my heart, but

when I first came to Glen Lyon I didn't think I had ever seen a place so beautiful as this," I said with a wistful sigh.

"Would ye like to stop here for a while?" he asked. "It's a lovely enough spot for our lunch."

"You're right," I agreed with a nod. "This is perfect."

We climbed down from the horses, Mr. Holme moving with some stiffness, and unpacked the saddle-bags. Together we spread out the extra plaid we had brought along to act as a blanket and unpacked the food we had packed.

As we arranged ourselves on the ground, I spread out the light fare of cold meats, cheeses and bread around us before revealing the bottle of wine.

"What's this, then?" he asked with a smile.

"I thought to bring it along so that we could celebrate," I told him.

"And just what is it we're celebrating on this fine afternoon, Miss Gordon?"

"Your health, of course. If that doesn't deserve celebrating, I don't know what does."

"You've a kind heart, Miss Gordon. I couldn't have been placed in better hands."

I could feel the warmth creeping up my neck at his flattery. "I didn't do much for you, truly."

"Ye kept me company and eased my pain. Ye took me in and watched over me." He reached out and took one of my hands in his. His eyes were riveted on mine and his gaze was intense, as if pleading with me to accept the sincerity of his words. "I am grateful to ye, Miss Gordon, for all that you've done."

"You're very welcome, Mr. Holme," I said softly, touched by his heartfelt declaration. "I'm glad that I've been able to be of some comfort you."

"It would please me greatly if ye were to call me Camden."

"I would like that as well. And you may call me Glenna."

He leaned in closer with a wide smile on his face. "I've been wanting to call you Glenna for days. You've a lovely name."

I laughed and removed my hand from his, slowly becoming aware that he had been holding it for a bit too long.

"Well, then, you can thank my grandmother, as I was named after her," I told him.

"I did have a question that I was thinking to ask ye, if ye don't mind."

I shrugged my shoulders and selected a small piece of cheese. "I suppose that all depends on what your question is," I said, then popped the morsel in my mouth.

"Fair enough," he said with a laugh. "I was wondering how ye came to be at Maggernie Castle."

I stilled and looked out over the long stretch of rolling hills, thinking carefully of how to answer the question. "I am a guest of the MacGregor. He and my father made a political arrangement ensuring peace between our lands," I explained.

"Ah," he said, his shoulder slumping ever so slightly. "So it's an arranged marriage, then."

"Not quite," I said with a smile.

He smiled at that. "I know it's dangerous of me to say it, but I must admit that I'm glad. I can't imagine how a woman as sweet as ye could be given to the MacGregor to wed. The man has a fearsome reputation. I have worried, these past few days, to think of ye under that man's control. I've yet to be introduced to him, but I can't say that I'm very sorry for it."

"He would never hurt me," I told Camden. "You needn't worry yourself."

"How can I not? Ye know as well as I the tales that follow that man. Every person in the highlands knows the kind of man he is. I would not see you fall victim to his foul temper."

I lowered my eyes and said nothing. I knew that Camden had nothing but true concern in his heart for me, but it still saddened me to hear the words. No matter how much I wished to correct him about Alastair's nature, it was not my place to do so. In fact, to disabuse Camden of his misplaced notions could do disastrous harm not only to Alastair but the entire MacGregor clan.

The stories and legends about the chiefs of the MacGregor clan went back farther than anyone could remember, and Alastair continued to cultivate them even to this day in order to protect his clan's most carefully guarded secret. Which meant that no matter how much it hurt my heart to say nothing, I could not speak out against Camden's beliefs regarding the man I loved.

"I'm sorry," he said. "I've upset ye, haven't I?"

"No, it's not your fault. It's a complicated situation."

"Well, you've a friend now, for as long as I'm here. I promise that I'll let no harm come to ye, Glenna."

I swallowed the lump that had formed in my throat and blinked back the tears that were threatening to surface. It felt so dishonest to deceive him this way when all he wanted was to look out for me.

"And you, Camden? I never did ask what brought you to Glen Lyon," I said, trying to change the subject. It was a clumsy attempt at best, but it was better than nothing.

"I was on my way home from visiting some cousins. I wanted to see something new and decided to test my luck by cutting through the MacGregor territory."

"And just look at how that turned out for you. Not quite the type of luck you were looking for, I suppose."

He reached his hand out as if to caress me, but stopped himself before he made contact.

"I would say that my rash decision was well-rewarded."

I blushed and looked away. I knew that I should say something, find some way to tell him that I was not free to give him my affections. It would be cruel of me to let him think that I was open to his advances. But there was nothing I could tell him that could be explained. Secrets upon lies—it was a horrible way to start a friendship but there was nothing else that I could do.

I would just have to find a way to discourage him without revealing the true nature of my relationship with Alastair. Camden would never understand, and more than that, the intimacy of my relationship with Alastair was enough to ruin me and destroy my good name. My love for him and my unwavering faith that we would eventually find a way to one day be wed were the only things that gave me strength enough to not fear the potential consequences of our actions. But we knew better than to flaunt our impropriety, even though the knowledge that we were not exactly chaste was probably the worst kept secret in all of Scotland. Though I knew it was cowardly of me, I did not want to risk learning how Camden would view me if he ever found out. It pained my heart to know that he would undoubtedly think less of me for it. The worst part was that I knew I wouldn't be able to blame him for it. Not one bit.

The next day I took Camden with me on my trip into Fortingall. He had insisted on coming with me when I had stopped to look in on him that morning. His movements around the bedchamber had been sure-footed and didn't seem to cause him any pain, so I couldn't see the harm in his coming along. Alastair had always insisted that I take one of his men along with me when I went into the village anyway, and with Camden coming along I didn't have to worry about taking anyone away from their regular duties so that they could escort me.

When we got to Iona's small house, Camden took the basket that I had packed for her with food from the kitchen at the keep. It would be nice to visit with both of them for a while.

I knocked on Iona's door but there was no answer.

"Maybe she's not home?" said Camden.

"That would be strange. I come to visit almost every Tuesday afternoon. She would be expecting me."

I knocked again and waited, but there was still no answer. Worry began to grow inside of me and I bit my lip as I considered what next to do.

"Do you think we should test to see if the door is locked?" I asked him.

Camden looked at me in surprise. "Don't ye think that's going a bit far? She's probably just stepped out. You're worrying yourself for nothing."

We turned to head back to the horses but I paused after a few steps to look back at the house.

"I'm sorry, Camden, I can't go yet. I have to know. She's elderly and lives all alone. What if she's fallen and needs help? I should at least look in, just on the off chance."

He nodded to me and started back toward the house. "All right, then, if you're sure."

"I am."

I tested the door and it opened easily.

"Iona?" I called, sticking my head through the doorway.

"It doesn't look like there's anyone here, Glenna. Let's go," he said, looking around the room.

"Not yet," I told him.

I pushed the door open and walked inside the house. The front room and kitchen were completely empty so I walked toward the back of the small house, where Iona's sleeping quarters were.

"Iona, are you home? It's Glenna." The door to her room was closed and I knocked on it softly. "Iona, are you in there? I'm coming in."

I opened the door to see Iona lying on her bed with her eyes closed.

"There, ye see?" said Camden from behind me. "She's sleeping. Now come away before ye wake her."

I stood rooted to the spot as I looked at Iona. Something was wrong. She was lying on the bed on top of her bedclothes instead of under them, fully dressed and with her shoes on. I walked into the room and a cold sweat broke out on the back of my neck. Iona's chest was perfectly still, when it should have had the steady rise and fall of breath.

I stood by her bedside and looked down at her. Her eyes were closed as if in sleep but her mouth was slightly ajar, with a tuft of fur protruding from between her lips.

I let out a muffled cry and turned away, burying my face in the protection of Camden's chest.

"My God," he said as he looked down at her. "Come away now, Glenna. Ye should not be here to see this. We must go at once."

I shook my head, pressing myself closer to him, unable to stop the tears that were streaming down my face. Iona had been one of the few friends I had made since coming to Glen Lyon. Though old and all alone, she had been a wise woman with a strong heart with many years left in her. For that time to be snatched away from her in such a cruel way was beyond comprehension.

Camden pulled me from the room and out of the house. I followed him on unsteady legs, the world around me a faint blur.

"This is three," I groaned.

"What?" asked Camden. "What do you mean?"

"Iona was not the first. This was the third time. The third... murder," I explained.

"There is a known murderer on the loose and ye came into the village today? Are ye mad, Glenna? What were ye thinking?"

"I was thinking about my friend!" I snapped at him. "What if I hadn't come today? Who knows how long it would have taken someone to find her. We don't even know how long she's been d-dead for," I stuttered, the tears coming harder again.

"There, now," he said, pulling me into his arms and holding me tightly. "That was insensitive of me. Of course ye wanted to look in on your friend. You've the heart of an angel, Glenna Gordon, and she was a lucky woman to have had ye for as long as she did. We'll make sure that she's seen to. Let's go tell the magistrate what's happened, then. He'll need to know."

I nodded and backed away from him, sniffling gently and brushing the tears away from my eyes. There would be time to mourn her later, but for now I had to let Mr. MacAlpin know that the murderer had struck again.

"I know where Mr. MacAlpin's office is," I said, my voice sore and raw. "Follow me."

The walk to the magistrate's office was the hardest I had ever taken. Each footstep felt as though my feet were weighed down by rocks, and the closer we got the heavier they felt. It was as if my entire body was in rebellion against the action I was about to take. Once we had told someone what had happened it would become real, instead of the waking nightmare I felt as though I were living in. Iona's death would soon be down on record, and there would be no taking it back. No erasing it. And no waking up.

I raised a heavy hand and knocked on the magistrate's door. The sound of it reverberated through me and I wrapped my arms around myself as we waited.

"Miss Gordon?" asked Mr. MacAlpin when he opened the door. He looked over Camden and me with curiosity. "What are you doing here?"

"It's happened again, Mr. MacAlpin," I told him. My voice sounded very faint and far away in my ears. "Iona is dead."

CHAPTER 18

"Glenna."

I looked up at the sound of Alastair's voice as he walked into the room. Mr. MacAlpin had sat Camden and me in his sitting room while he went to investigate the scene at Iona's home. I could not go back there; the pain of seeing her body again would have been unbearable. So the magistrate had sent word to Alastair back at the castle about what had happened and left us in his home while he attended to his duties. Camden and I had been sitting in heavy silence for hours.

"Alastair," I said with a sigh of relief at the sight of him.

"So it's true, then," he said as he crossed the room to me. "Are ye all right? The message said that ye found her."

I nodded sadly and tried to hold back another wave of tears.

"Ah, love, come here." He opened his arms to me and I rushed into them, so grateful that he was there.

"It's all right now, I've got ye. I promise ye it'll be all right."

I looked up at him with watery eyes and he brushed my hair away from my face. Then, using his thumb, he wiped away the tears from beneath my eyes.

There was a sound of shuffling from behind me and I remembered that Camden was still in the room with us. Alastair looked at him over the top of my head and I turned awkwardly to face him. The moment Alastair had entered the room I had forgotten everything else, and I had no explanation to give.

Camden stood up and took a step toward us, his hand outstretched to Alastair. "Camden Holme," he said by way of introduction.

"Alastair MacGregor." Alastair shook the smaller man's hand as he examined him. "Chief of Clan MacGregor. It's good to see ye on your feet and looking so well, Mr. Holme."

Camden started at the introduction, confusion flashing in his eyes as they traveled to me for a split second and then back to Alastair.

"We can thank Miss Gordon for the speed of my recovery. She was very good to me," he told Alastair.

"Aye, she's a soft heart. It was good of ye to stay here with her."

"I wouldn't dream of letting her out of my sight," said Camden.

Alastair didn't respond, but he shifted slightly in front of me, partially blocking me from Camden's view. I looked back and forth between them as they eyed each other silently. Alastair had a slight frown on his face, and I wondered if he had a sense of Camden's interest in me. I had not told him about what had transpired on our ride the day before. I had not been able to see any good coming from the revelation.

"Do you have to go to Iona's house now?" I asked Alastair, trying to break the tension that was growing palpable in the room.

"Yes," he said with a nod, "but I wanted to look in on ye first. Though now that I'm here, I don't want to leave ye," he said softly, reaching out to take my hand.

"No, you have to go take care of this. I have to have justice for Iona. We cannot let whoever is committing these crimes get away with it. It's Iona, Alastair," I pleaded with him. "You must find this person."

He cupped my cheek in his hand and I closed my eyes, leaning into the comfort of his touch. It no longer mattered to me what Camden thought. I loved Alastair and I needed him near me.

"I will find them, Glenna, I promise ye that."

"I will take her back," said Camden. "There is no need for her to stay here now. I will escort her back to the keep."

Alastair clenched his jaw before nodding. "Aye, that would probably be best."

"I don't want to leave you," I said.

"I know, love, but ye must. I will be back with ye as soon as I can."

"All right," I agreed with a sigh.

"Mr. Holme," said Alastair to Cameron, "I would be very much obliged to ye if you were to keep an eye on Miss Gordon this afternoon. See that no harm comes to her."

"Aye, I'll guard her with my life."

Alastair jerked his head in a nod, and with a last look to me he strode out the door.

Once he had gone I sat back down heavily in the chair I had formerly occupied. While I was ready to be out of the magistrate's sitting room, I was not yet ready for the long ride back to the castle, as it was sure to either be full of questions from Camden or worse, none at all.

"So, that is the MacGregor," he said mildly, his eyes still on the doorway that Alastair had just walked through.

"Yes."

"He's quite... tall," he continued.

"Yes, I suppose he is, at that."

"He seems very fond of ye...."

I looked at my lap as my fingers moved idly, pleating the fabric of my gown. "Yes."

"But you're not engaged to be wed?" he asked.

"Not officially, no." This evasive line of questioning was even worse than I had thought it would be.

"And unofficially?" he pressed.

"Unofficially? Well, that's a bit more complicated."

He nodded and stood up, extending his hand to me. "It's been a hard day. We should be getting back."

I nodded and accepted his hand. He helped me out of the chair and we left the magistrate's offices.

The ride back to the keep was a silent one, each of us lost in our own thoughts. I wanted to say something to keep a distance from growing between us. Something that could make him understand why I had such affection for a man Camden must consider to be the devil himself. But I could not think of the words. So I stayed silent and tried to accept the inevitable loss of two friends on the same day.

The sun had long gone down on the day when there was a soft knock on the door of my bedchamber. Alastair had stayed in the village for the rest of the day, and had not been back in time for the evening meal. I had gathered my courage and went to find Camden to see if he would join me for dinner in the great hall. Thankfully he had greeted me with a smile, with no sense of distance between us.

I walked to the door and opened it to find a very tired-looking Alastair standing on the other side.

"I wasn't sure if I would see you this evening," I told him as he entered.

"I told ye that I would come for ye. Did ye think I would let you down?"

I shook my head and drew him deeper into the room.

Alastair sat on the bed and removed his boots, letting them drop heavily to the floor before lying back on the pillows.

"Come lie with me a while, Glenna. I'd have ye near me."

I curled up next to him on the bed, resting my head on his chest as his arm came around me.

"I'm sorry for your loss, love. Iona should not have met her end that way."

"She was so wonderful," I told him. "I confided so much in her. She was my first true friend since I came to stay here."

"I am sorry that it has taken people so long to warm to ye."

"It's not their fault. It must be very confusing for them to have me here. They are all very polite, but I don't think they quite know what to do with me, and so are very cautious. And how can I blame them? I may be Glenna Gordon today, but at any time I could be Lady Glenna MacGregor. I think they fear becoming overly familiar. But I believe that I may still be able to count Mr. Holme as a friend, though I was very doubtful of it earlier today. I was grateful that there was no awkwardness between us at dinner."

"He has an eye for ye, Glenna," said Alastair, his voice a low rumble.

"I know," I said quietly.

"And ye trust him, then?"

"He has been kind to me, Alastair. I do not encourage him, but I do welcome his friendship."

"To know ye is to love ye, Glenna. I cannot fault him for falling for ye. But I also canna say that I like it."

I looked up at him and smiled. "Are you saying that you're jealous?" I teased him.

"No, I am not," he said with a huff.

I laughed, my heart feeling a bit lighter. "I do believe you are. You're jealous, the fearsome Alastair MacGregor. Will wonders never cease?"

Grabbing me, Alastair pulled me bodily on top of him, his arms wrapped around my waist, and held me tight.

"Oh, aye? And what have I to be jealous of, then? You're mine, Glenna Gordon. I know that just as I know that the heart that beats in my chest beats for ye. I've no need to be jealous, for I know where your love lies. He can pine after ye all he wishes. I care not, so long as it goes no further than that." He pulled me close and kissed me swiftly. "Or maybe I should mark ye as my own, so that he knows just how taken ye are, aye?"

I squirmed as he nuzzled into my neck, the rough bristles of his beard tickling my sensitive skin. He kissed me softly, but soon the gentle caress of his lips turned more forceful as his mouth widened and he bit me gently, the pressure of his teeth slowly increasing as he suckled on the area. The feel of him demanded my attention, and I allowed him to distract me from my sorrow, if only for a little while.

"Maybe I'll give ye a love bite so bold that it can be seen straight across the great hall. Leaving no doubt in anyone's mind just to whom ye belong."

His words thrilled me. I had never thought that I would be attracted to a man who showed such posses-siveness. Never thought that it would make me feel so safe or cherished to hear such sentiment.

Alastair pressed a gentle kiss to my shoulder and rolled us so that I was on my back and he half-covered me with his body.

His large, sure hands traveled down the length of my side and over the gentle flare of my hips before coming to rest on the generous curve of my backside.

"Have I ever told ye how much I love the feel of ye, lass?" he asked me as his hand gave me a firm squeeze.

"No, I don't think you have." I flushed warmly.

"Aye," he said with a lazy smile.

His hand moved back around to my hip and up to cup my breast.

"And these?" he asked, squeezing the soft, full globe. "Have I told ye how very fond I am of these?"

The heat in my body continued to rise and I shook my head.

His hand left my breast and he brushed his thumb across the fullness of my bottom lip.

"And your lips? Have I also forgotten to tell you how sweet they are?"

My lips parted slightly and his thumb slipped between them. Going on instinct, I bit down gently on the tip of it, and was rewarded with the flash of hunger I saw in his eyes. Encouraged by his reaction, I closed my lips around it and ran my tongue over the digit as I watched his face closely.

His throat bobbed as he swallowed and I could hear a low growl coming from deep in his throat, so I decide to bite his thumb a little harder.

His eyes fluttered closed for a moment and I heard him take a sharp inhale of breath.

"That's a dangerous game you're playing, love," his said, his voice a low rumble.

I reluctantly released his thumb. He was right: this was a dangerous game. One that was getting harder and harder for us to play.

CHAPTER 19

I had a late start to the day the next morning. My heart was still aching over the loss of Iona and I had ended up sleeping well into the late morning as I gathered the strength to face the day. I had to fight the urge to lie in bed all day wrapped in my sadness. I knew that no matter how I felt, Iona would not have wanted me to wallow in the sorrow of missing her.

I forced myself to wash and dress for the day, then made my way to the library. I hoped that burying myself in a good book for a few hours would serve as a decent distraction until I felt ready to face the rest of the day.

It wasn't until I had the door to the library partially open that I realized the room was already occupied. Disappointed with the discovery, I began to close the door, not yet ready for company, but I paused when I heard Mr. MacAlpin's voice raised in anger coming from inside.

"This is completely unacceptable, MacGregor, and we will no longer stand for it," Mr. MacAlpin said.

"I'm sorry ye feel that way, Mr. MacAlpin, truly I do, but my decision stands," said Alastair. His voice was firm, but he sounded weary, as if this were a conversation they'd had many times before.

"It will not stand," the magistrate insisted. "Ye have a duty to your people, sir. Do ye deny that?"

"No, Mr. MacAlpin, I do not. But I would hope that I had earned the trust of my people by now. I'd hoped that all of those who stand with ye on this would reconsider in time, in light of all I had done."

"Reconsider? When every day ye put the future of this entire clan at risk? No, MacGregor. If you continue to insist on marrying this woman, I warn ye, ye will have a war on your hands."

I heard shifting from inside the room and then Alastair's voice came, low and menacing. "Are ye threatening me, Mr. MacAlpin? Maybe ye think ye would be better suited as chief, aye?"

I heard Mr. MacAlpin swallow audibly and I almost felt sorry for the man.

"I have no intention of challenging ye for the position of chief, MacGregor, but I will not deny that there are those more than willing to step forward if you do not make the choice to do your duty by your people. I know you love Miss Gordon, but a union between the two of ye is impossible. It is time for her to leave. Ye must send her away."

"Mr. MacAlpin, you've made your position on the matter more than clear. Now let me try to make myself just as transparent. I love Miss Gordon and I will not be sending her away, not now, or ever. Ye may be the magistrate but I am still chief of this clan until such a time as I die or someone challenges me for the position and wins. And I'll warn ye now, MacAlpin, if ye do find someone to challenge me, I have no intention of losing. I do not take kindly to your bringing such division to my people."

"Ye brought this division upon yourself the moment ye insisted on taking this woman as your own, MacGregor. Don't blame me for your ill judgment. Your stubborn love for this woman will tear our clan to pieces. And then what will ye do? Is she truly worth that? Is she worth the destruction of everything that we've worked so hard to build? Bodies in the streets, MacGregor! Bodies in the streets and the threat of war within the clan. Ye must do something to control this clan. Unless ye want to be known as the chief that let his clan fall to ruin while he buried his head in the sand and his cock in a—"

I jumped at the sound of Alastair's fist coming down hard on something.

"Finish that sentence, MacAlpin, and I'll be forced to remove your tongue from your throat," Alastair told him, his voice low and menacing.

"Yes, well." Mr. MacAlpin coughed, "I believe ye take my meaning."

"All too well," Alastair growled. "Now, MacAlpin, if ye dinna mind, I have many things to be seeing to. Ye know your way out."

"Mind my words, MacGregor, and do the right thing."

I had heard more than enough and closed the door as quietly as possible before hurrying away.

Every day that I stayed, I was driving a wedge into the middle of this clan. I loved Alastair with all my heart and I had believed that together we could overcome anything. But maybe we were simply fooling ourselves. Were we just being selfish by insisting on staying together? Could I honestly say that our happiness was more important than the stability of the entire clan? No, I couldn't. The honorable thing for me to do would be to leave, to simply make the choice for both of us and leave before this got any harder and the fighting got any worse. There was no other way.

I snuck a small bag of food upstairs from the kitchen and dumped it on the bed. I had to move quickly so as not to be discovered. It wasn't unusual for me to be seen carrying baskets around the castle when I was on my way into Fortingall, so no one would look too closely at my actions, but I did not want to push my luck, either. The faster I was packed and on the road away from the keep, the better for everyone.

I hurried to the wardrobe, pulled out my cloak and wrapped it around my shoulders. I didn't bother to pack an extra gown, as it would be a long ride back to the Gordon lands and I would need to travel lightly. I would have everything I needed when I was back on my father's land.

The chamber door opened behind me as I was fastening my cloak and I spun around to face a confused-looking Alastair.

His eyes roamed over me as he took in my traveling attire and spotted the saddlebag on the bed.

"Are ye going for a ride, love?" he asked.

"I... yes, I am," I stuttered. "I thought a bit of fresh air would do me some good today."

"Aye." He nodded slowly. His eyes narrowed as he examined my face and looked at the saddlebag again.

"Who's going with ye, then?" he asked.

"I... I thought to go by myself today. It's silly that I always have to inconvenience one of the men whenever I want to go riding."

"Ye know it's not safe for ye to be riding out there alone, Glenna, especially now. If ye insist on going for a ride right now, then I'll go with ye."

"But..."

The look he leveled at me just then silenced me in an instant and I simply nodded.

"Fetch your bag, then," he said quietly, then waited for me to walk ahead of him out the door.

The horses were saddled quickly and we were soon on the road, riding in silence away from the keep.

"Here," he said after a while. "Our lake isn't far from here. Why don't we stop there for a bit?"

"All right."

We directed our horses off the main road and into the trees. Before long we came to the edge of a deep blue body of water. Alastair had brought me to the lake for the first time when I had first arrived at the castle, leading me here in the middle of the night while in his wolf form. It was that night that everything had changed between us, though I hadn't known it then. My heart constricted at the memory and I had to fight back my tears.

After we'd dismounted we walked to the water's edge and looked out at the still depths. Alastair stood behind me on the bank but did not touch me. I was not stupid; I knew that something was wrong. He seemed distant from me and I worried that his fight with Mr. MacAlpin had taken its toll.

"Were ye even going to say goodbye?" he whispered.

The pain in his voice reached deep inside me and crushed my heart. I should have known that he would see straight through me. What had made me think that I could deceive him?

"I was going to write you a letter..." I said sadly.

"A letter," he repeated coolly. "I suppose that's better

than nothing. At least ye were not going to disappear without a trace and leave me wondering. I should be grateful for that, aye?"

It sounded so insulting. A letter. After all that we had shared.

"I could never do that to you," I told him. I kept my back to him, still unable to turn around and face him.

"Oh, aye, of course," he scoffed. "But ye could sneak off and leave me like a thief in the night."

I closed my eyes and lowered my head. Every word was like another blow to my heart.

"I was trying to do what I thought was best," I said weakly.

"What ye thought was best?" he snarled.

I cried out as he grabbed me roughly by my arm and spun me around to face him. I flinched away from the look of pain in his beautiful green eyes. It killed me to know that I was the one who had put it there.

"How, Glenna?" he demanded. He took me by the shoulders and shook me until my teeth rattled. "How could ye think that that was what's best?"

"Stop, Alastair, stop!" I wrenched myself from his grip and stumbled away. I pressed a hand up against a tree to steady my balance as the tears began to flow. I wanted so badly to do the right thing, but seeing the pain that my leaving was causing him I was no longer certain what the right thing was.

"It's not fair," I yelled. Turning to him, I brushed roughly at my tears, determined to stay the course. "It's not fair what my being here is doing to everyone. If I go, it's over, it's done. I'm the problem, Alastair. Me. And if I go, things between you and your people will go back to the way they should be. My leaving will hurt for a while, I know, but you'll move on in time. Our hearts will heal."

"Ye think it will hurt for a while? Hurt for a while!" he roared. "You're tearing my heart out, Glenna, can't ye see that? And it'll not heal in time because there'll be nothing left of it! Did ye think ye could just go off and leave me with naught but a letter to soothe my wounds and think that I wouldn't hunt ye down and drag ye back to my side where ye belong? Do ye truly think that there is a world in which I would be willing to give ye up?"

He stormed toward me and pressed me back against the tree. His unleashed anger engulfed me and it felt as if the heat of it burned all the air out of the woods, I could barely breathe.

"I just want to do what's right, Alastair. We've been so selfish."

"I dinna care! Everything I have ever done, I have done for them. But not this time. This time I will keep what's mine."

He pulled me to him and kissed me, pouring all of his anger and frustration into our embrace. I struggled to find my footing. I felt as if I were drowning in his need.

His hands were everywhere, grabbing, squeezing

and tugging at me, trying to take hold of as much of me as he could. He lifted the skirts of my gown to my waist, then, cupping me, he lifted me up and pressed me hard to the tree. My hair got caught on the rough bark and snagged painfully, but I did not care. I wrapped my legs around him for support and kissed him back just as madly. Any thoughts of leaving had been wiped completely from my mind.

He was right, of course. How could I have ever thought that I would be able to walk away from him?

"You'll not be leaving again, ye hear me?" he growled into my ear.

I nodded, panting, as I tried to catch my breath.

"Say it," he demanded.

"I'll not leave again," I promised.

"Say it again."

"I swear I'll not leave you again."

He captured my mouth again but this time more gently, his early fury slowly abating as he set me back on the ground. I clung to him, not yet ready for us to be parted. I needed to keep touching him. I had been so close to losing him. So close to walking away. And it would have been the worst mistake I had ever made.

"Ye must stop scaring me like this, Glenna," he said gently as he stroked my cheek.

"I'm sorry," I told him with a smile. "I'll not do it again."

"Will ye come home with me now?"

"Aye," I nodded. "I'd like that very much."

As I climbed back up into the saddle and settled myself I looked over at him as he mounted his horse.

"How did you know?" I asked him.

"That ye were leaving? I didn't at first," he said. "I knew ye were at the door when MacAlpin was there, love. I knew ye had heard what he said and I wanted to come check on ye to make sure ye were all right."

"You knew I was there?"

"Aye. I know the smell of ye, Glenna. I'll always know when you're around. I'll always find ye, love, and I'll always protect ye. I promise ye that. Now, let's go home."

CHAPTER 20

*D*ays passed and the hurt between Alastair and me healed. He understood why I had done what I did and quickly forgave me for the pain that I had caused him.

I was so wrapped up in my love for him and my joy at being back that it took me a while to notice that Camden had been strangely quiet. It wasn't until I was sitting with him at supper one evening that I truly noticed it. He replied to my questions with short one or two word answers, which was completely unlike his usual animated banter. The more he continued to look sullen and withdrawn, the more I was worried that something was very wrong.

I knocked on the door to Camden's chamber and entered before waiting for his reply. "Camden?" I asked hesitantly.

"Glenna, I'm glad that you're here," he said, coming

over to greet me. "I have something that I wish to discuss with ye."

A pained expression had replaced the usual sparkle in his eye, and worry settled in the pit of my stomach.

"Is everything all right, Camden? You did not seem yourself earlier."

"I've had much on my mind the last few days, Glenna, and after a lot of thought I've finally come to a decision, though it does not come easily to me."

"Oh, Camden, what is it? You have me worried now. Whatever is the matter?"

He took my hand and drew me over to the window chair where he indicated for me to take a seat. My heart hammered as I sat down and he paced back and forth in front of me. I had never seen him so agitated before.

"Camden, please, you're beginning to scare me."

"I'm sorry, Glenna," he said, taking up my hand in his again as he squatted down in front of me. "I did not know how to tell ye and it's been eating away at my mind, but I have decided that it is time for me to leave here and travel home."

"Oh, Camden, so soon?" I asked sadly.

"Yes. I have long since recovered from my injuries and in truth I should have left days ago. But ye see, I could not bring myself to leave your side."

His hands squeezed mine tightly as he stared deeply into my eyes.

"Oh, Camden..."

"Please, Glenna. I love ye. I know it must seem impossible and much too soon but I canna deny how I feel."

"We are friends, Camden," I said carefully, "and with that of course comes a certain amount of affection."

He shook his head and pressed the palm of my hand flat against his chest, holding it tightly there with both of his hands. I could feel the intense hammering of his heart beneath his shirt.

"Do ye feel that, Glenna Gordon? The way my heart pounds? I need nothing more than to think of your sweet face before my heart starts hammering so. It is not mere affection I feel for ye, lass. I have never felt this way about anyone in my life. I knew ye were the one the first time I set eyes on ye."

"Oh, Camden, I can't... I don't know what to say." My mind was a blur as I tried to come up with some way to let him down gently. To explain to him that I did not feel the same way for him without breaking his heart.

"Say ye feel it as well, this connection between us," he pleaded. "Say ye love me as I love ye."

"Camden, I'm sorry," I whispered, "but I cannot."

Pain flashed in his eyes and his hands gripped mine so tightly that I winced. "Do not say that, Glenna. I know that it canna be true. I know ye love me too. Ye must," he insisted.

"Camden, I am so sorry, truly I am. I am not free to love you. You have been such a good friend to me, and

I would not want to lose that friendship. I have not meant to deceive you in any way. But my heart belongs to another. I love the MacGregor. I love Alastair."

"He has ye bewitched, Glenna. Can ye not see that? How else could someone with a heart as sweet and generous as yours love such a man? He is a monster. Ye know just as well as I the legacy that man carries. And ye expect me to believe that ye would give yourself to such a creature of your own free will? That ye would go willingly to his bed?"

"Camden!" I gasped, shocked that he would mention such intimacies.

"Ye have been blinded, Glenna!" he hissed. "Ye may not be able to see it, but I can. I do. Come with me."

The pain in my hand was getting worse and I tried to tug it away, but he held me too tightly.

"Camden, please, that hurts," I sad, tugging again. My sympathy for him was rapidly turning to unease.

"Come with me, Glenna, I beg of ye. I will take ye away from this place. All that is before you is darkness and pain. How will ye hold your sweet head up with pride anywhere in Scotland once ye are wed to that beast? He is feared everywhere. His unprecedented cruelty is known by all. Once ye are his, he will snuff the light from ye. All that ye are, all that shines bright and true, will be stripped from ye until ye are an empty husk. Come with me, and I will give ye everything you deserve. I will give ye a life of happiness and light. I will love ye, Glenna. I will love ye like no other man ever will."

"Camden, please," I begged. "You must stop this. You don't know what you're saying. I canna go with you. I will not go with you." I looked him in the eye and tried to keep my voice from shaking. "I do not love you."

"I don't believe ye," he insisted, and he released my hand to grab my shoulders. He pulled me to him and pressed his mouth hard against mine.

I froze for a moment in complete shock before it gave way to anger and I struggled against him, pulling my mouth away from his. "Camden, no! You are confused. This is not you," I snapped at him.

"I love ye, Glenna. I love ye," he said frantically, his eyes wild.

He pulled me back to him kissing me roughly. His tongue probed at my lips, seeking entrance as I tried to keep them closed to him. I turned my head away in disgust as my fury flared up inside me.

Wrenching myself away, I reared back and slapped him across the face, the sound of the impact cracking through the room.

Camden released me and took a step back, raising his hand to the bright red spot on his cheek. He looked at me with dead eyes as he lowered his hand. "So that's how it's going to be, then," he said, his voice flat and devoid of emotion. Every hint of the love-struck man had been erased.

"Yes," I said, my chest heaving, "it is. I had hoped

that when it came time for you to leave that we would part as friends. But I see now that is impossible. I believe that it would be best if you left at once."

He sighed and shook his head. "This would have been so much easier if ye had just come with me out of love, Glenna. It would have been much more comfortable for ye, at least at first. Unfortunately that's impossible now. I'm sorry, lass, but what comes next is not going to be nearly as pleasant for ye."

A cold dread flowed over me at his words and I took a step backwards as he advanced on me. "I don't understand," I told him. My eyes flickered quickly to the doorway and back again.

"I was told that ye weren't very bright, but I didn't think it would be so hard to turn ye away from the MacGregor. Ye seemed like a woman more accustomed to gentle words than being manhandled by a brute. But it looks like I was wrong. Maybe this would have worked if I had just been rough with ye from the beginning."

The blood froze in my veins as his arm lashed out and he grabbed hold of my wrist, tugging me toward him. His other hand snaked up into my hair and he wrenched my head back, the pain of it making my eyes water.

"So is that it, Glenna? Do ye like it rough, then?" he asked.

The next thing I knew, Camden was throwing me against the wall. I fell to my knees, and my head bounced off the edge of the table on the way down. I knelt there shaking as I saw his boots advance on me.

"Come now, Glenna, show a little spirit. I'd hate to believe that you're really as pathetic as I was told," he said with a laugh.

"Why are you doing this?" I yelled, shocked by his sudden venom.

"Why?" He laughed, and a shiver went down my spine.

I cried out as he grabbed me by the hair and dragged me across the floor to the center of the room, then he released me roughly, shoving my head down to the floor.

He dropped to his knees and rolled me over, pinning me beneath him. As I looked up into his face I did not recognize the man I saw there. Gone was my friend, and in his place a stranger looked out from his eyes. I tried to sit up and pull myself away, but it was no use.

Camden slapped me and my face exploded in pain. I swung out at him, but he grabbed my wrists while he straddled me, sitting on my legs to keep me from kicking out.

"There it is," he said with a laugh. "Looks like you've got a little fire in ye after all. Not such a gentle angel, are ye?"

"Get off of me!" I yelled, struggling to free myself from his grip.

He leaned over and kissed me, trying once more to

shove his tongue into my mouth. I tried to turn my head away, but he grabbed my face and squeezed it tightly. This time I opened my mouth and allowed him entrance, but the moment I felt the invasion I bit down hard.

Camden yelled and wrenched his head away. I was expecting his slap this time, and it only fueled my anger. I opened my mouth to scream, but the sound was cut off by his hand.

"Now, we'll have none of that," he said menacingly. "Ye should have run faster."

Taking hold of the front of my dress, he wrenched it at the seam, tearing open the front and exposing one of my breasts. I bucked wildly, and the blood pounding in my ears was all that I could hear. This couldn't possibly be happening to me.

"Come on now, love," he snarled. "I'm not trying to take anything that you haven't already freely given that beast MacGregor. If you'll let a devil like that spread your dimpled knees, what's one more, aye?"

With a surge of strength I tore one of my hands free and punched him in the nose as hard as possible. There was a sickening crunch and blood began to pour from it.

He yelled and released me, his hands flying to his face. With a mighty shove I toppled him off of me and I ran for the chamber door. Holding the torn ends of my dress to my chest, I ran down the empty hallway. My slippered feet echoed softly in the dark, with my light footsteps soon followed by his heavier ones.

I pulled on a door only to find it locked, and continued running. The second door I tried opened under the force of my hand and I dashed inside, slammed it closed behind me and barred it. A hard thud came a moment later and I jumped, then backed away slowly, never taking my eyes from the door.

"Let me in, Glenna!" he shouted, and a moment later he pounded again. "Let me in, ye stupid wee whore!" There was a heavier thud from lower down where he must have been kicking the door but it held fast.

After that I heard nothing as the long minutes crawled by. I crept closer to the door, trying to not make a sound as I listened for movement on the other side.

"I will find ye, Glenna." Camden's voice was a low, menacing hiss. "I will find ye and I will kill ye. MacGregor will die. Everyone in this castle will die. And I will find out the names of every friend ye have and I will kill them just as I killed your precious Iona."

My hands flew to my mouth as I tried to hold back a gasp, and my body shook violently, but I continued to walk toward the door until I was standing a hair's breadth from it.

"Riding into town and killing her really was the perfect way to spend the afternoon after that lovely picnic ye and I shared. We are coming for ye and we will wipe every demon-spawned mutt born to this clan from the land," he spat.

He punched the door, the blow of it landing right where my face was, and I jumped back as if freed from a trance. A moment later I heard his heavy footfalls as he ran away from the door.

I rushed to the far corner of the room and crouched down in the corner, my face buried in my knees, too afraid to leave.

CHAPTER 21

I don't know how long I sat there in the dark, too scared to leave the room for fear that Camden was still lurking outside the door. His words echoed over and over again in my head. Somehow he knew—he knew about the curse of the wolf on clan MacGregor, and he wasn't alone.

Eventually I heard the muffled sound of footsteps outside the door and I froze, afraid that it was Camden come back again. The voices slowly became more clear, among them a low, rumbling voice filled with worry that I recognized as Alastair's.

"Have ye not seen her at all then, Donald? She didn't mention that she was leaving?"

"She's not left the keep, Alastair. Someone would have seen her go."

I unfolded myself from the corner and stood on shaky, weak legs. "Alastair." My voice was tight and raw and came out barely above a whisper. I stumbled toward the door and hurried to unbar it. "Alastair," I said again, louder this time as I fell into the hallway.

"Glenna?" He and Donald were already some distance down the hall, and he turned to look back.

Clutching the torn ends of my dress to my chest I ran to him, tears streaming down my face. As I got closer I could see him taking in my appearance. The expression on his face grew from confused to murderous.

"Oh, Alastair!" I threw myself against him and he wrapped me in his arms.

"Glenna, what's happened to ye?" he demanded.

"It was Camden," I told him, my voice filled with shame and simmering anger. "He deceived me." I shook my head and looked up at him. "He told me that he loved me, that he wanted me to run away with him. And when I refused him, he changed. He said the most awful things and he... he tried to force himself on me." I whispered the last, still feeling the greasy shame of the encounter.

Alastair stood very still as if struck from stone. "Donald?" he said, his voice dripping with ice.

"Yes, sir?" said Donald, who stood shaking beside him, hands clenched at his sides.

"Gather the men. Tell them we are going hunting."

"Right away," said Donald. The older man turned and left us standing in the hall.

"This way, Glenna," Alastair said.

"Alastair, wait. There is more," I said as he led me away.

"It can wait, love. Let's get you seen to first."

He hurried me through the castle. Very few people were wandering the halls, most of them already gone to their beds. But Alastair blocked me from what few eyes were around to see me in my state of undress and shame.

When we got to my bedchamber I turned to him and slapped a hand to his chest to stop him. Rage had been growing in him the entire way there and I needed him to hear what I had to say.

"Alastair, please stop. I need you to listen to me."

"I should have been here to protect ye," he growled. "I should have sensed the type of man he was. I should never have let him anywhere near ye."

"Alastair, what happened to me wasn't your fault. And I'm fine. I got away."

"But he laid hands on ye!" Alastair exploded. "He tried to force himself on ye! And he bruised ye..." He reached out and touched my face lightly and I winced away from his touch. The skin on my face was more tender than I had realized. "I'll kill him." He turned to head for the door.

"Alastair, stop!" I shouted.

So very rarely did I raise my voice at him that he turned and looked back at me in surprise. The last time it had happened we had been fighting in his study over whether or not he would meet my father and his men on the battlefield in war. I had been decidedly against it.

"Alastair, you will stop right there and listen to what I have to say," I demanded.

"What is it?" he asked impatiently. His hands clenched and unclenched at his sides as though eager to feel Camden's neck against their palms.

"He knows, Alastair," I said.

"Knows what?"

"He knows about you, the wolves, all of it. He knows of the curse."

"How is that possible?" He strode back to me, alarmed. "What did he say?"

I closed my eyes, remembering. "He said that he would kill all of us. You, me, everyone. That your people were evil. Demons. He said that he wasn't working alone and that they were coming to destroy us. Oh, Alastair, he said that he killed Iona."

"He will pay for it, Glenna. I will make sure that he drowns in his own blood."

"No," I told him.

"Don't be ridiculous. What do you mean, no?" he scowled.

"You heard me. Do not kill him. I want you to bring him back here. Bring him to me, Alastair," I told him firmly.

"I am not letting him anywhere near ye. He will never see your face or speak your name again!" he shouted.

I looked up at him and squared my shoulders. His eyes were deep green and flashed with rage. I knew that he was willing to do whatever it took to protect me, but I needed this. I needed to see Camden again.

"You will bring him to me, Alastair, and you will bring him to me alive. After what he's done... I was so scared. I need to face him. I have to. I cannot let his face be the one that haunts my nightmares. Please, Alastair, do this for me."

He reached out and pulled me to him and kissed me fiercely. I melted into his touch, the feel of him banishing the last wisps of fear that had kept their grip on me.

"I will do this, if this is what it will take for you to be free of him."

"Thank you. Now give me a moment to change."

"I must go, Glenna. We are running out of time."

I ran to the wardrobe and discarded the torn gown on the floor before pulling out the first gown I set my hand on. When I pulled it out it happened to be a deep crimson red. The color felt very fitting. I dressed as quickly as possible.

"All right, I'm ready," I told him, and we rushed out the door.

When we got to the courtyard, about twenty men were standing there waiting for Alastair and many of them seemed surprised to see me. I recognized most of their faces not only from seeing them around the keep but also because most of these men had been there in the woods when my uncle had traded me to Alastair in the middle of the night, a few short months ago.

These men had seen me when I was at my most terrified and humiliated. It was almost a relief that they were the ones to stand before me now.

Alastair stepped forward holding a sheet that he had stopped to tear off the bed Camden had been sleeping in. He tossed it out to his men, who caught it eagerly.

"What you're smelling is Camden Holme," he shouted loudly as they passed the sheet among them, burying their faces in the fabric so that they could inhale the scent.

The air felt full, like just before a storm, and the hair on my arms stood on end.

"That man came into our home under a false guise. Took advantage of our hospitality. Murdered our people. And attacked the woman who would be my wife!" he roared. "Hunt him! Find him! But bring him back alive!"

The tension in the yard was palpable as the men began stripping down, tearing off their clothes with little regard for my presence. I watched as they, to a man, stood naked before me. Their bodies started to shift and contort. Then their limbs began to elongate and the nails on their hands grew into long, vicious-looking claws.

Soon the men were gone and in their place were giant wolves. I reached out and stroked the familiar soft black coat of the beast that was Alastair. Just like when he was a man, he was larger than the rest of the wolves before him.

The pack threw back their heads and howled as one at the moon. The sound of it poured over my skin, crashing over me like a wave. Camden would never make it out of the area alive. Of that I had no doubt. They would find him, and they would bring him pain.

I watched as the wolves took off into the trees and disappeared like shadows. A peace settled over me as they disappeared one by one. There was nothing for me to do now but wait.

I paced back and forth in Alastair's study for the better part of three hours before I heard a loud commotion in the hallway. It wasn't long before the door to the study burst open and Alastair strode forward. His plaid was in disarray, betraying how hastily he had redressed himself after shifting back to human form. Behind him, Camden Holme was being dragged between Donald and Gregory.

Alastair stood beside me and together we watched as the men threw Camden down on the floor in front of them. I thought that I would feel something at the sight of him. Fear, anger, or disgust. Instead, I found myself devoid of all emotion. I examined him with cool disinterest. He had obviously been beaten very badly.

His lip was newly split, and someone had re-bloodied his nose. There was no doubt now that it was broken. Kneeling before me, he cradled his hand to his chest and blood trickled through his fingers.

"What is wrong with his hand?" I asked.

"One of the men took two of his fingers," said Donald smugly.

I raised my eyebrow at this, but Donald simply shrugged and said nothing more.

"Well, you wanted him alive, Glenna. He's alive. Ye said nothing about him being whole," said Alastair gruffly.

"Oh, I don't mind," I told him, my voice flat and emotionless. "I was merely curious."

Camden eyed me and chuckled. "Look at ye now, Glenna. So brave. Ye weren't nearly this calm when I had ye on your whore back. I see you're much stronger with the MacGregor at your side."

I took a step forward, but Donald beat me to him and kicked him swiftly in the ribs.

"The only reason we didn't tear ye limb from limb when we found ye is because Miss Gordon wished it," Donald said.

Camden chuckled again and winced as he came to his knees. "Sounds as if sweet Glenna is more fond of me than she would care to admit."

Alastair stepped forward but I put a hand on his arm to stop him. I still needed Camden alive.

"How did you find out about us?" I asked the man I had once called friend.

"Ye have enemies who know your secret. They were more than willing to share it with those they thought would have the best chance of bringing ye down."

"I have always had enemies," Alastair told him. But none among them would have known about our curse to tell.

Camden shook his head and smirked. "No, not you, MacGregor. Her," he said, nodding in my direction. "Our sweet Glenna has made someone very, very angry. So angry, in fact, that they are determined to destroy the entire MacGregor clan and all ye hold dear. After that it didn't take much for them to find people to help bring ye MacGregors down. Your people haven't made many friends over the last few centuries, have ye?"

"Who would do this?" I asked. "Who would hate me so much that they would do this to us? I have harmed no one!"

"Are ye sure about that, now, lass? Because Allina wanted me to pass on the message that she looks forward to seeing ye again very soon."

The blood froze in my veins. There was no way what he was saying could be true.

"Allina is dead," I told him. "I saw her killed with my own eyes."

"Did ye stop to check? Because she's obviously not

so dead as ye might think. That little lass is holding quite the grudge against ye."

"She would destroy her own people out of petty jealously?" I hissed, not believing what it was I was hearing.

He shrugged as casually as possible while wincing in pain. "I dinna care what it was that drove her to do what she did. All that matters to me is that my people now have what we need to hunt ye down and wipe your cursed existence off the face of the earth. Your days are numbered, MacGregor. We're coming for ye."

"We are not afraid of ye," Alastair told him. "If your people bring war to mine, they will be crushed."

"I seriously doubt that your true name is Holme," I said. "Who are you, really?"

"Ye expect me to tell ye that? No, you'll find out soon enough," he said.

"Give me your dirk," I said to Alastair, holding out my hand.

"Glenna..." he said, his voice unsure.

I said nothing, but simply kept my hand extended until he placed the hilt of his long knife against my palm.

The two clansmen hauled Camden upright and held his head by his hair so that he was forced to look me in the eye.

"Are ye going to kill me, then, Glenna? I don't think ye have it in ye. Little angel, you're much too sweet."

I pressed the long dagger against his throat and

applied some pressure. Doubt flickered in his eyes and I leaned closer to whisper in his ear.

"You should have run faster."

I took the knife from his throat and plunged it into his gut. Leaning away, I kept hold of the knife and watched as the life drained from his eyes. I did not remove it until I was sure I had heard the last breath leave his body. Then I stepped back and stood up straight.

"Get him out of my sight," I told Alastair's men.

Donald nodded, and the two men picked up the body of the man I had once known as Camden Holme and carried it out the door.

CHAPTER 22

"*A*re ye all right?" Alastair asked me. He placed his hand on my shoulder and turned me to face him.

"I think..." I paused to consider for a moment and took a shaky breath. "I think I am. I'm tired of being weak. I want to be able to defend myself and the people I love. I want to be able to defend your people. Our people."

"Glenna, I've never thought of ye as weak. You've always had a fire in ye that I admire."

"I want you to bite me," I told him.

He took his hand from my shoulder and took a step back. "No. Ye don't know what you're asking."

"I do know, and I'm not asking you lightly. I want us to be together. Properly, as man and wife. I want to stand beside you and bear your children and help you to protect these lands from whoever is coming our way."

"Glenna, I could not do that to ye."

"Why not? We could finally be together. Completely. We would no longer have to fight to be together. We could be wed." I took his hand in mine and brought it to my lips. "We could be one."

"Glenna, love, when you're bit the change is painful. It is very, very painful. I would not put ye through that. And more than that, not every one who's bit completes the change. Not everyone makes it through to the other side. Sometimes people go mad. Their minds canna handle it. Or they simply die from the pain of it."

"I am strong enough for it, Alastair, I know that I am," I pleaded with him. "Do not deny me this chance to be with you. Whatever the pain. I will endure it if it means that we can be together."

Alastair's face was awash in conflicting emotions, and I prayed for him to agree to my request. I knew that he wanted nothing more than to keep me safe, but this was what I wanted. And I wanted it more than anything I had ever desired before in my life.

He lifted my hand and kissed its palm, then reached out with his free hand and caressed my cheek.

"Glenna Gordon, I've loved ye from the first moment I saw ye. You're the most loving, brave and beautiful woman I know. I would be honored to spend the rest of my life with ye, lass. And if turning ye is what it takes and you're certain that it's what ye wish, then that's what we shall do. So what do ye say? Will ye marry me, Glenna, and spend the rest of your days with the dreaded MacGregor? Will ye be my wife and mate?"

My heart swelled with love for him and I launched myself into his arms, bursting with joy. "Aye!" I shouted with laughter. "Aye, Alastair, I will marry you and I will love you until the end of my days and beyond."

He lifted me off the floor and pressed a long, lingering kiss to my lips, his long red hair forming a flaming halo around his grinning face.

It amazed me that an evening that had started with such horror could end with so much joy.

Later that night Alastair and I awoke to the sound of insistent pounding on the chamber door. The room was still dark, with no sign of the early morning sun on the horizon. We must have only been asleep for a few hours.

"Sir, miss, ye must come quickly," came Donald's harassed voice through the door.

I rubbed the sleep from my eyes and hurried to dress myself in my nightgown before wrapping a plaid around my shoulders for modesty's sake. Alastair dressed in naught but his kilt, and opened the door to face a red-faced Donald.

"I'm sorry to have awakened ye, but there's been a

messenger. He insisted that I wake ye both at once. He's brought a package with him."

"Where is it?" Alastair asked him as we quickly followed him.

"In your study. Gregory is watching the messenger in there as well," Donald explained.

"Did he say who it came from?" I asked.

"No, my lady, he didn't. But with the threats against us I thought it best to keep him here for questioning for the time being."

The lamps had been lit in the study by the time we arrived and a short young man cloaked in black sat in one of the leather chairs. Gregory, the clansman who had been with us in the library when Camden had been brought before me, was watching him suspiciously.

"Who are ye, and what brings ye here in the middle of the night?" Alastair asked the stranger, dispensing with the niceties.

The man—a boy, really, for he looked little older than seventeen years of age—stood and looked toward the wooden box that sat on the large desk.

"I was sent here with a message for ye, MacGregor," he said.

"And just who is this message from?" Alastair asked him.

"I have no name for ye," the boy told him.

"Do ye expect me to believe that you rode here to deliver me this message without knowing from where it came?" Alastair took a menacing step forward and glared down his nose at the boy. "Or maybe ye simply require some persuading to tell me what ye ken?" he asked quietly.

The boy swallowed audibly but did not back down. I admired his courage, but it would not help him if Alastair decided that he was a threat. The safety of the clan came first, always. And now we all had to be more careful than ever.

"Ye do not scare me, MacGregor," the boy said with only the barest of quivers in his voice. Then, suddenly, moving quickly, the boy produced a knife and slashed out at Alastair.

Alastair lifted his arm to defend himself from the strike and the knife slashed into his forearm. Ignoring whatever pain the wound must have caused, he moved without hesitation, and reaching out with both hands he took hold of the boy's head and twisted it sharply to the side, effectively snapping his neck.

I watched wide-eyed as the lifeless body of the boy fell to the floor. My eyes traveled from the boy to Alastair and back again, my heart full of sadness. This was not the first time I had seen Alastair take a life. He had protected me from another like him, a man cursed with the wolf, paid by Allina to assassinate me. But I had never seen him take a human life before, and for it to be one so young, even if the boy had been an assassin, shook me.

"For them to send a boy to try to kill me," Alastair said, shaking his head. "They had to know he would fail." He looked down at the boy's body, an expression of extreme regret on his face.

"I dinna think he was meant to succeed," said Gregory. "More likely he was meant to be another mark against ye. A spark in this war they're determined to bring to our door."

"Aye, Gregory, you're probably right," Alastair said, his voice tight with frustration. He walked around his desk and opened drawers until he located a handkerchief, which he pressed to his arm to stanch the blood flow.

"What about the box?" I asked. I walked over to the large, hinged box and placed a hand lightly on the lid.

It was well crafted. The wood was a deep, rich brown and well oiled. The metal hinges were of an intricate knotted design, and there was no mistaking the fact that it was obviously very valuable.

"Shall I open it?" I asked, looking over my shoulder at the three men. My fingers were already tracing the seam around the edge of the box and I began to lift the lid.

"Glenna, wait," said Alastair, but it was too late.

I tossed the lid back and looked down. "My God!" I gasped.

The men came over to examine the contents of the box.

"Damn them!" Donald yelled, kicking the desk in his anger. Then, glancing over at me, he added, "Pardon my language, lass."

The palms of my hands had gone damp but I reached over and grasped his hand anyway.

"Damn them," I whispered in agreement.

"Come away, Glenna," said Alastair.

"No," I told him as I continued to stare into the box. I could feel something inside myself hardening at the sight of it, as if an invisible wall were being built around my heart. It had truly begun. They were coming for us. And with this declaration of war, I knew without a doubt that I would do whatever it took to defend my new family and fight by their side.

The wolf had been a natural-born one, not someone with the curse. I knew this not only due to the comparatively small size of the wolf's head resting in the box, but by the fact that it was the head of a wolf. If it had been a clan member, then the body would have reverted to human form upon death.

We could breathe a little easier in the knowledge that this was not someone we had known sitting before us. It was a small consolation in the light of things, but a welcome one.

"Why is it covered in tar?" I asked, confused. The wolf's fur was tangled and matted, liberally streaked through with black.

Alastair leaned forward and inhaled. "To mask the scent," he said. "See how the inside of the box is coated in it as well? He pressed a finger to the inside of the wooden box and tested the tackiness of the dark substance. "The tar masked the smell of the wolf. The boy never would have gotten inside the keep otherwise."

"Do ye think that's why it was so difficult to track Camden and whoever was helping him with the murders? They were covering up their scent like this?" asked Gregory.

"They must have been. It's the only thing that makes sense," agreed Alastair.

"I want you to do it now," I said quietly.

"Are ye sure this is the time?" Alastair asked, understanding my meaning completely.

"There will never be a better time," I told him. "Do it."

"Donald, Gregory, I'd ask ye to excuse us, please."

"No," I said, stopping them before turning back to Alastair. "I would have them witness this. I want there to be no doubt. No question."

"It would be an honor, miss," said Donald, bowing low to me.

"Aye," said Gregory, giving me a sharp nod.

Alastair looked at me with a mixture of hope and trepidation in his eyes as he began to remove his plaid, slowly unwrapping the pleated folds of his kilt. I could feel the warmth rising in my cheeks. I had seen him get undressed countless times before, and I had watched as he and his men disrobed and shifted as a group. But this, now, in the hushed silence of his study, seemed even more intimate than all of those times put together, especially with both Donald and Gregory looking on.

Alastair looked into my eyes as the last of the fabric fell away and landed with a soft thump on the study floor. I held his gaze intently as he began to shift, until standing before me was a giant black wolf.

The beat of my heart kicked up as I looked at him. My fear of him in his animal form had been dispelled long ago, but as I gazed upon him now I could not help focusing on the sheer size of his massive jaws. He had to bite me with those jaws, and I did not see how he would be able to manage it without removing one of my limbs completely.

"Hop yourself up on the desk there, lass, and shift to the side a bit so he can get your thigh," Donald offered, sensing my concern.

I swallowed and nodded. I sat on the edge of the desk with my legs dangling over the edge and turned to the side.

"Now, if you'll just, umm... lift your skirts a bit," he continued. His face went just as red as I was sure mine was. "A little higher, now. There ye are."

The gathered fabric of my skirt pooled at the top of my thigh, exposing the entirety of my leg. I stared down at the unmarked skin of my thigh and then looked to the wolf that was Alastair. He padded forward slowly but stopped before reaching me. Waiting, he tilted his head to the side, as if to ask one last time if I was sure that this was what I wanted. I held out my hand to him and he closed the distance between us, allowing me to run my hands over the familiar, comforting feeling of his fur.

When I had first arrived, the wolf had been my only friend, my companion as well as my guard, and I had come to care for it. Then, when I learned that the wolf was Alastair, I came to love the man. Neither man nor wolf had ever hurt me nor brought me harm, and as I touched his soft coat, I knew that there was naught to fear from him now.

"I'm ready," I told him, my voice strong and sure.

The wolf threw his head back and howled, then moved very quickly and wrapped his jaw around the soft flesh of my upper thigh. Pain like fire shot through my leg but I did not cry out. My hands clenched into tight fists and my nails dug into my palms but I did not make a sound, and his sharp teeth were gone from me almost as quickly as they had broken the skin.

Dazed, I looked down at the bite and noticed that it was surprisingly shallow as blood began to well up. Donald and Gregory hurried forward, but I shook my head. I did not need their help. Grabbing the edge of my wrap, I pressed it to my leg, stanching the flow on both sides.

It was over. I was bitten. I couldn't believe that it had finally happened.

"Glenna," came Alastair's voice.

The sound of his voice made me jump. I had not even noticed that he had shifted back.

"It is done," I whispered in wonder. "I thought there would be more pain, but it is passing already. The bite almost feels cool now."

Alastair looked stricken, and I noticed Donald and Gregory exchange quick glances.

"What is it?" I asked. "What is wrong?"

Alastair gathered me into his arms and held me tightly, pressing my face against the warm skin of his chest.

"I am so sorry, Glenna, my love, but it is not over yet," he said into my hair.

"What do you mean? I am bitten..." I trailed off as the cold in my leg began to intensify and spread. "Alastair?" I asked uncertainly.

"I am sorry!" he cried through clenched teeth.

The cold grew and tore through me like the fierce bite of winter, burning me from the inside, but the very worst of it was centered in my thigh, a cold that burned so intensely that I was sure the flesh would melt from my bones and fall to earth as chunks of ice.

"Alastair!" I screamed as I clutched at him, shaking uncontrollably.

All I could feel was ice and fire as my body shook and jerked, and then the world went black.

***

I awoke to the welcome feeling of a cool cloth pressed to my forehead. I was unbearably hot and shifted uncomfortably.

"There now, love. You'll be all right now," crooned Alastair in a low, hushed voice.

I reached for him and he grasped my hand, then kissed it over and over again.

"I am very hot," I croaked. My voice was raw and hoarse, my mouth dry.

"It will pass. The fever is breaking," he reassured me.

"How long have I been like this?"

"Three days," he told me. "Your fever was much worse than I anticipated. We are so close to the full moon. I should have waited until it had passed."

"No, I am glad that we did it now. We can be together for always now."

He smiled at me, his eyes filled with love, and set the cloth aside.

"Glenna, ye mean more to me than words can ever say. I never thought the day would come when I would find the woman who completed me, and then one night there ye were. I would have gladly gone to the ends of the earth for ye if it meant that we could be together."

"I know you would have. But I love you too much to ever ask you to make that kind of sacrifice for me. Do not regret what has happened here, Alastair, please. I wanted this."

He shook his head and leaned over me, pressed a soft kiss to my lips, then rested his forehead against my own.

"I don't know which is greater, lass, the guilt I feel

about the pain I've caused ye, or the guilt I feel about how joyous I've been these past three days, even as ye lay here suffering. Because I knew that ye would awaken and be mine, and that not even God in heaven could take ye from me now."

I grabbed Alastair's face in my hands and let the joy pour out of me as I kissed him. I understood his words completely, because I felt the same way. There was nothing in heaven or on earth that would be strong enough to tear us apart. A storm was coming for us, that much was certain. But we would face whatever was in store for us side by side.

CHAPTER 23

The highland air was warm and the summer moon was large above the thick, lush canopy of the forest. It was only a few nights past the full moon, but even without its bright silver light I would have been able to see the world around me as clearly as if it were midday. Twigs snapped easily beneath my paws as I ran free, my large, powerful body weaving through the trees and over the rolling hills behind the keep. I had never felt as free as I did at that very moment.

As I ran, I could hear the sounds of the night world around me. Sounds that I had been deaf to before the blood of the wolf began to pump through my veins. An owl hooted loudly up above, and I glanced up to watch it take flight from a branch high above me into the clear night sky. Its dark shape crossed over the face of the moon before it vanished out of sight.

As I crested the hill I stopped to look back at the dark, imposing shape of the keep below. Meggernie Castle. I sat back on my hind legs and raised my head to the sky to sniff at the air before letting out a single long howl. Then I crouched low and propelled my body forward as I sped back toward the keep, my home, and Alastair.

I came to a stop just before the thinning edge of the trees that surrounded the castle and looked around for any clansmen who might be out walking the grounds late at night, keeping watch. Finding the coast clear, I took a deep breath and shifted back into human form. Shifting the first time had been painful, my body taking its new shape only a few short nights after Alastair had bitten me. I'd thought that I was going to die from the pain of it, the way my body bent as every bone broke and realigned itself into wolf form. But after that first change the shifts had started to come easier and more fluidly over the next month.

I took a deep breath as I stood up from a crouch and let the fresh air caress my naked body. I was in no rush to clothe myself. Running as a wolf was the most freeing thing I had ever experienced and I had become loath to rejoin the world of man after an enjoyable midnight run.

With a deep sigh, I slipped the simple forest green

gown over my head and started for the doors of the keep, pausing for only a moment to wave to the watchmen once they were within sight to let them know that I had returned safely.

It was well past midnight as I climbed the stairs to my bedchamber. The castle was quiet, with only a handful of people roaming the halls. I turned the corner and crept down the hallway as quickly and quietly as possible. I was sure that Alastair was still asleep in my chamber, and it wouldn't do me any good to wake him and be caught sneaking back into the room in the middle of the night.

I slipped into my chamber and closed the door softly, breathing a sigh of relief.

"Did ye have a good run, then?" a rough voice asked me from the dark shadows of the bed.

Closing my eyes with a soft sigh, I turned in the direction of the voice to face Alastair. "Yes, thank you, it was lovely," I told him.

"Oh, aye? Good, good," he said casually. Too casually. "Because ye know I would hate for anything to interrupt your runs. Ye know how irritating those assassination attempts can be."

"Now, Alastair," I said, hoping to soothe him before he got too angry with me. "I was careful. It was perfectly safe."

"Perfectly safe!" he exploded. Throwing back the covers, he stood up and stormed toward me wearing naught but his loose nightshirt. I could only barely make out his face in the sliver of light that came through the seam in the shutters of the window, but that was all I needed to see that his expression was thunderous. "This is the third time, Glenna. The third time you've snuck off in the middle of the night to go running. Ye know that we're all in danger and yet off ye go without a moment's notice and taking your life in your hands. Have ye so little love for me, then?"

"How could you possibly ask me that?" I gasped, his words a blow. "You know I love you more than anything. After all we've been through, how could you possibly doubt that?"

"Because I'm trying to understand why ye would do this time and again if ye had any care for me at all. I wake up and find ye missing, your side of the bed gone cold. And I don't know if you've gone to find something to eat or if you're lying dead in the woods somewhere with an assassin's arrow stuck in your side!"

My shoulders drooped and I hung my head in shame. "I'm sorry," I said quietly.

Alastair sighed heavily and pulled me into his arms, wrapping them tightly around me. Cocooned within his warmth I grasped the back of his shirt, feeling the strong muscles of his back against my hands, and rested my head against his broad chest.

"I understand the call, lass," he whispered. "To hear the wild call to ye and for your blood to cry out in answer. It's strong, and 'tis a connection that ye will now feel for the rest of your life. It can be tempting to spend more and more time in wolf form, but ye must take care."

"I know, Alastair. I know that it's a dangerous time, and my rational mind tells me that I'm taking such a stupid risk... but then the wolf calls to me. I can feel her inside of me aching to get out and I find myself giving in, and it's wondrous. I've never felt so free. How do you stop? How do you control it?"

"It takes some practice but it will get easier with time, I promise." He was quiet for a moment before asking, "Where did you run?"

"I didn't go far, just up the hill behind the keep, then back again. I just wanted to stretch my legs."

Alastair chuckled and bent over to kiss the top of my head before releasing me. "Am I going to have to keep a closer eye on you?"

"No," I told him, shaking my head emphatically. "I won't sneak out again, I promise. You're right. I have to be smarter and learn to control my urge to shift."

"I'm not trying to cage ye, love, and if I've the time I'll run with ye if ye ask me. But we have to prepare. War is coming, I've no doubt of it, and we need to be ready. We can't afford to be caught unaware another time. Whomever Allina has found to carry out her vengeance has proven to be strong and cunning. We cannot allow them to get the upper hand."

"I know, Alastair. I understand. I'm sorry for causing you so much worry. Has there been any news?"

I moved to the wardrobe and stripped out of my

gown, exchanging it for a plain white shift that I slipped into before crawling under the covers of the large bed. Alastair walked around to the other side and slid in next to me, pulled me into his arms and settled back.

I raised my hand to my mouth to stifle a yawn as my eyelids started to flutter closed. The late hour and the run had taken more out of me than I had thought, and sleep was beginning to quickly overtake me.

"The men that I sent out to the neighboring clan lands haven't sent back any news of use yet. There have been no murmurs from the Grahams, Stewarts or MacLarens," he told me, his voice weary.

"Have heart, Alastair. We are sure to hear something soon. Don't worry. Allina is a spiteful woman, and she may have found allies in order to play out her vengeance against us, but you will find a way to protect this clan just as you always have. I have no doubt of that. There will be news soon. Have faith."

Squeezing me close, Alastair pressed a kiss to my lips. "Aye love, you're probably right," he said, closing his eyes. "We can only wait and see what the morning brings."

"I know all too well what the morning brings. I had hoped to be able to put it off for another day, but it has been long enough and it is time. The clan has to know."

~

Alastair and I walked silently hand in hand toward the great hall. I had awoken early that morning despite my late night run, my stomach full of anticipation as I dressed myself and attended to my hair. I had moved the comb slowly through my locks as I stared out the window, half lost in thought until Alastair tapped me gently on the shoulder and informed me that it was time for us to go downstairs.

The great hall was loud and hectic that morning, and the long wooden tables were surrounded by men, women and children crammed onto the benches side by side as they readied themselves for the long day ahead.

I paused at the entrance to the hall in order to take a final steadying breath before squaring my shoulders and walking toward the dais at Alastair's side.

Ever since the official announcement of our engagement, the castle inhabitants had slowly begun to open up to me, no longer eyeing me with an air of suspicion. But even more than the engagement, it was the whispers of my change that seemed to have cemented my place in the clan. The fact that I had allowed Alastair to bite me was the reassurance the people had needed to put their trust in me and to finally welcome me into the MacGregor clan—but the news Alastair was about to tell them could easily undo all of that.

Alastair stood before the head table and silently stared out across the room. One by one the occupants began to fall silent, the first ones to notice Alastair's call to attention quickly silencing the others around them.

I stood a few steps behind him and off to the side, offering my support as the woman who was to be his wife. The clan sat patiently waiting for him to speak, and I watched as their eyes flicked to me every so often. A sober reminder that not only were these people a clan, but a pack. More tightly woven than any family.

"I come to you this morning with grave news." Alastair's deep voice boomed out around the hall. "This clan has been betrayed by one of our own." He paused as the room exploded into murmurs before lifting his hand for order. "Allina MacGregor has betrayed us, and has told someone of our greatest secret. This clan has seen too much death these last months. Death carried out by those whom Allina has enlisted to try to break us."

"Why would she do this?" someone asked. "How could she turn her back on her own?"

My hands balled into fists and I clenched my teeth together so tightly that I started to feel a pain in my jaw as I prayed that Alastair would not give them those details.

"The why of that matters not," he told them. "All that matters is that she sent not one but two murderers into our midst. One who attempted to kill me in my study last month."

"But that is suicide!" a woman cried.

"Yes," Alastair said gravely, "it was. And they both paid for their folly with their lives. You all know that the man calling himself Holme was responsible for the killings in Fortingall and I am telling you now that he will not be the last. More will come for us. They will seek us out and hunt us down. We must be prepared for an attack."

"This is unheard of!" a man cried from the crowd. "For centuries we have remained hidden, and now all of a sudden everything that we have worked for is at risk? I do not believe that anyone in this clan would betray us in such a way. What proof have you that Allina betrayed us like this?"

Alastair's hands clenched and unclenched as I watched him struggle with deciding how much to tell his people. I took a deep breath and stepped forward beside him. He glanced at me, a look of surprise on his face, and I nodded to him, accepting that he needed to tell them why their secret was now out.

"Madness has taken Allina," he told his people. "This madness drove her to not only try to have Glenna killed but to bring her vengeance down upon all of us."

"So it is the human's fault!" a woman wailed. "No good can come of this! This is what comes of trusting outsiders."

"The fault lies with Allina and her alone. She has chosen her actions and she will be brought to justice for them. Glenna Gordon has proven her loyalty to me and this clan time and again, and I will not hear of any blame being placed upon her shoulders. Glenna is soon to be Lady MacGregor and I would see you show her the same loyalty and respect that you have shown me."

Even as heads nodded I could hear a low rumbling of unhappy murmurs within the crowd and my stomach sank. It felt as if no matter what I did, something happened to put a rift between me and the MacGregor clan, and I wondered if there was anything that I could do to earn their trust. I needed them to believe in me, especially in the troubled days ahead.

CHAPTER 24

*A*lastair and I rode into Fortingall that afternoon with his uncle Donald and clansman Gregory. Although I had eventually gotten my way, it had taken some persuading on my part for Alastair to agree to let me ride into the village with them. He believed that I would be safer in the keep in case there was an attack, but I had assured him that there was no safer place for me than by his side, and that if we were to be wed I needed to continue to take any opportunity I could to interact with the people in the village.

While that was mostly the truth, there was no denying that I was also simply desperate for a change of scenery, even if it was just a short ride down to the village.

Everywhere I had gone in the castle that morning I had found myself being followed by curious eyes, and I couldn't help but wonder if they were asking themselves if the blame for this was something that could be laid at my door. It would not have been the first battle that the MacGregors had found themselves needing to fight due to me, so was it so far-fetched that I was somehow at the center of this latest disaster? It must have felt like I had brought them nothing but trouble from the moment Alastair had brought me to the castle.

As we got closer to the town square I saw a large crowd gathered around. There was a lot of shouting, with people calling over one another, trying to be heard. From the back of my horse I was able to see over the heads of the crowd to the center of the group, where a large, dark-haired man seemed to be riling up the crowd.

"We need to stand strong. We need to take care of our own, because the MacGregor, up there in his castle isn't going to take care of us!" he shouted.

I gasped at his words and my eyes flashed over to Alastair, wondering if he had heard what the man had said.

Alastair sat straight up in the saddle. The knuckles on his hands were bone white from the tight grip he had on the reins.

I turned back to the large man in the center of the crowd to listen to what he had to say.

"We MacGregors have always been feared throughout the highlands for as long as we can remember. We have been the thing of whispers and nightmares. We have held respect! Our mystery has protected us throughout time and our curse, this wolf blood that flows in our veins, has been ours alone. But now what do we have? We have a chief who that takes an outsider as his wife and who is so vulnerable that he was attacked in his own keep! Have we grown so fat, so lazy that the other clans are now welcome to simply murder us in our own beds? What are we to do with a leader who can no longer lead? Are we going to stand for this? Is this how we will be remembered by our children? By our children's children? And if we do nothing, say nothing, will we even last long enough to have those sweet bairns and to teach them our ways? To see our wolf pups howl at the moon and take them for their first hunt? We may be a clan, but are we a pack? And if we are not, then who is to blame?"

The crowd grew louder, a mix of encouraging cries at the man's words and angry grumbles of agreement.

As I watched him whip the crowd into a mutinous frenzy, my mind raced as it tried to make sense of what he was saying and how he could be so insanely foolish.

"What is going on here?" Alastair called out.

The heads in the crowds turned as one and the masses hurriedly stepped back as their chief slowly rode toward them. They parted like the sea, making way for him to pass until he was directly in front of the speaker.

Alastair swung himself down from his horse and

looked the other man squarely in the eye. "What is your name?" he asked the man gravely.

"Graham McConnell, sir," the man replied. He stood tall, his back straight, and it suddenly struck me that this was the first man I had ever seen who could rival Alastair in height. Over time I had gotten used to Alastair's size as I was so often near him, but now I stood in slight awe of the two men who towered over the crowd around them. They looked like giants, and I feared for those who would be crushed if these two came to blows.

"What is it that you're trying to accomplish here, Mr. McConnell?" Alastair asked him mildly, his eyes never leaving the other man's.

"I want the people of this clan to take a hard look at where they've found themselves," McConnell told him, his voice unwavering. "We are a strong, proud people, and yet we act as if we were the hunted instead of the hunters. We have grown lazy and as tame as the common hound instead of as wild and free as the fierce creatures we are. We have untold strength and power, and yet we squander it. We have stayed hidden so long that the wolf blood that flows through us is turning to dust in our veins. We must break free. We must rally together and show our strength. The days for hiding are over."

McConnell finished his speech and raised his chin defiantly, as if he were daring Alastair to strike him, his body tense and ready for the blow. But Alastair did no such thing.

"If ye believe that ye can lead this clan better than I have done these many years, then ye know what ye must do. But I warn ye, if ye take such action against me, it will be folly," Alastair snarled.

McConnell blinked at him in surprise before silently bowing his head.

"As I thought," said Alastair before turning his back on McConnell and mounting his horse.

I watched as to a man, each person in the square followed McConnell's lead and silently bowed their heads to Alastair as we rode by. I breathed a sigh of relief, thankful that Alastair had been able to put a stop to the trouble before things had gotten out of hand.

"Should we be worried?" I asked Alastair as we continued on our way to Mr. MacAlpin's house.

"I'm not sure yet," he told me. His eyes narrowed, focusing on the road ahead.

"I don't like the way he was riling up the crowd. He could be a problem," I continued.

"I think I made my point very clear, but you're right. He could pose more of a problem in the future," Alastair agreed.

When we arrived at the magistrate's house, we were

greeted by his housekeeper and ushered inside to the sitting room.

"My lord, Ms. Gordon, a pleasure as always," Mr. MacAlpin said with a deep bow and a smile that did not quite reach his eyes.

"MacAlpin," said Alastair, distracted, with a curt nod of his head. His attention was obviously still on the scene we had just witnessed outside.

I stepped forward to greet the magistrate with a wide smile. "Mr. MacAlpin, how nice it is to see you. I hope you've been well."

"Yes, Miss Gordon, very well, thank ye. We've been having a fine summer, don't you agree?"

"Yes, very fine," I agreed, already growing bored with the niceties that were necessary before we got down to the task at hand.

I highly doubted that Mr. MacAlpin and I would ever grow to like one another. He had been much too vocal about his distaste for Alastair's wedding me and I didn't think that he would ever fully approve of me.

Mr. MacAlpin's housekeeper poured our tea for us as we got settled. Alastair waited until the door to the room had closed softly behind her before he allowed himself to tell Mr. MacAlpin exactly what was on his mind.

"Mr. MacAlpin, are ye or are ye not the magistrate of this area?" Alastair asked him mildly.

Unsure of himself, Mr. MacAlpin looked around at the other men in the room but was met with a sea of black faces. "Yes, MacGregor, I am," he said, shifting uncomfortably in his seat.

"Then why, I wonder, is there a mob gathered outside within shouting distance of your door, questioning my leadership and the future of our clan?"

I watched the magistrate with interest as he swallowed audibly.

"Well, ye see, MacGregor, I suppose I felt the people had a right to voice their concerns..." He trailed off lamely at the sight of the storm clouds gathering on Alastair's face.

"I see," Alastair said with a nod. "Ye thought they should be able to voice their concerns, did ye? And ye thought that they should be able to voice those concerns without you there to make sure things dinna get out of control?"

"They... they didn't seem overly violent or... disrespectful when they first started to gather," Mr. MacAlpin stuttered.

It amazed me that the man had ever been appointed to office. I wondered vaguely how much money must have changed hands for him to secure his position, because I couldn't see how he could have been appointed as magistrate due to any great show of competency.

"MaccAlpin, I came to speak to ye today so that we could discuss how we would work together to keep these people calm in this troubling time. But from what

I saw out there, I am seriously beginning to question your ability to do your job effectively."

"I can assure ye, MacGregor, that I do my job and I do my job well. And if ye are displeased with my performance, then maybe ye should just find someone else to appoint as magistrate," he said with great boldness.

Mr. MacAlpin's eyes went wide, as if he was only just realizing what he had said, and he hurried to continue before Alastair could take him up on his offer.

"Of course, I remind ye that I have been magistrate in the area since your father was chief. If he had questions or doubts about my ability to perform my tasks efficiently, then I would have been replaced long ago."

"Though that may be, Mr. MacAlpin," said Alastair, "I think it would be unwise to make any drastic changes just yet. The future is unsure enough without giving our clan more to worry about. But I expect ye to get a firmer handle on what's going on out there. The last thing we need is rioting in the street."

"Of course, sir, of course. I will endeavor to put an end to any more of these gatherings before they've begun. Now is the time for peace and order while we prepare to defend ourselves from the enemy at the gates, not squabbling amongst ourselves like errant children."

Alastair sighed and pinched the bridge of his nose in frustration. "Just be sure to keep the people calm, Mr. MacAlpin."

The magistrate flushed red but held himself straight, bristling in indignation. His eyes flickered toward me, and my eyes flickered away from him as I took a sip of tea. I suddenly found myself very interested in the lovely floral pattern around the rim of his teacup. Out of the corner of my eye I saw the magistrate flush an even deeper shade of red and I knew that any displeasure he felt toward me was only being deepened by the fact that I was here to witness Alastair voicing his displeasure with the man.

"Alright, enough of this," said Alastair. "Mr. MacAlpin, why don't ye tell me what you've been working on with the outlying crofters? Has word of the threat been sufficiently spread?"

Sitting back, I listed intently as Alastair and the other men discussed the actions that would need to be taken to prepare for any further attacks from Allina.

CHAPTER 25

*T*he sunshine streamed in through the open shutters of my bedchamber window as I lay in the soft cocoon of blankets, staring up at the ceiling. I raised a trembling hand to my breast and could feel my heart pounding in my chest.

There was a soft knock on the door and I sat up in bed. "Hello?" I called.

"It's Anna, Miss Glenna. I'm here to help ye get ready."

Shaking, I threw back the bedcovers and walked slowly toward the door. Taking a deep breath, I took hold of the handle before opening the door wide.

"Thank you, Anna. Please come in."

As I stepped aside to allow the maid entrance, my gaze landed on the ivory gown hanging from my wardrobe door and my heart skipped a beat. It was finally happening. I was about to marry Alastair.

The morning moved by in a blur as Anna dressed my hair and helped me into my gown.

"You look lovely, miss," said Anna. Our eyes met in the mirror as she smiled at me. "You're the most beautiful bride I've ever seen."

"Thank you, Anna," I said softly, with a nervous smile.

She rested a hand on my shoulder and gave it a gentle, reassuring squeeze.

Our moment was interrupted by a firm knock on the door.

"I'll answer it for ye, miss."

Anna walked over to the door and opened it to reveal my father.

"Da!" I shouted. I leapt up from my chair and rushed over to the door. "Oh, I've missed you." I squeezed him tightly.

"Glenna, lass, let me take a look at ye, my girl." He took me by the shoulders and held me at arm's length so he could look me up and down. "Ye look good, lass. I'm glad to see ye looking so well."

"Thank you, Da. I'm so nervous."

"Are ye having second thoughts?" he asked me, a slight frown touching his face.

"No, not at all," I reassured him. "I've never been so certain of anything before in my life. I just... I can't believe it's finally happening."

"I didn't want to let ye go, that day ye told me that ye

were choosing to stay with the MacGregor. But to see ye standing here in front of me now… You're such a vision, my girl. The spitting image of your mother the day I married her. Well, my heart is just filled to bursting."

I could feel my eyes tearing up and I pulled my father close, resting my head on his shoulder. "I wish she could be with me here today. I miss her."

"I miss her too, lass, and I know she's here with ye today watching over ye. She wouldn't miss seeing ye wed for all the world."

I took a deep, shaky breath and gave him a watery smile, then I brushed my hands down over the skirt of my wedding gown to smooth out the non-existent wrinkles while I collected myself. "Where's Fin?" I asked him, curious about the absence of my little brother.

"He's around here somewhere, terrorizing the MacGregor's men with what must be a thousand questions, but I know he's eager to see ye."

"I wish that I could speak with him now," I told my father. I hadn't seen either of them in months and I was eager for the visit.

"You'll see him soon enough. But first it's time to get ye to the chapel so that ye can be wed. Ye don't want to keep your future husband waiting, now, do ye?"

"I cannot believe that it's already time."

"Aye, lass, it's time." My father took my hand and

tucked it into the crook of his arm, then escorted me out of the room.

My mind raced as we headed toward the chapel. As we got closer I could hear music from inside spilling out into the hallway through the closed double doors and my heartbeat doubled its pace.

We stood before the door and my father patted my hand. "Are ye sure about this, lass? Because if you're not..."

"I'm sure, Da. I've never been more sure of anything before in my life."

I looked at the two men standing on either side of the door and gave them a nod. They smiled at me and nodded back before they each took hold of a door handle and opened the doors to the chapel.

I took a step forward and gasped at the sight. The chapel had been filled with beautiful flowers and the pews were filled with the castle's inhabitants. But all of that faded and fell away as soon as I set eyes on Alastair at the end of the aisle.

I took a slow step forward and then another. It soon felt as though I was moving automatically, drawn toward him. At the end of the aisle I turned to my father, who kissed me softly on both cheeks, a touch of moisture shining at the corner of his eye. He took a seat in the front pew next to my brother Flynn, who was grinning widely as he waved at me. I grinned back at him before turning to face Father MacGregor.

Alastair took my hand in his as the priest began to

speak. We stared into each other's eyes as we recited our vows, promising to love each other until the end of time. In no time at all Father MacGregor had declared us man and wife, and I was in Alastair's arms as I kissed him for the first time as his wife.

I was only vaguely aware of the cheers that went up around us as the world disappeared and there was only the two of us left.

The great hall was filled to bursting as our wedding guests danced and laughed and toasted to our happiness. I threw back my head in merriment as I reeled with my younger brother Flynn, whirling around the dance floor with carefree abandon.

Our dance came to an abrupt stop as I turned to find Alastair standing directly in front of me.

"Master Fin, I hope you'll excuse me the intrusion, but I was hoping to have this next dance with my wife," he said to my brother with an incline of his head.

Fin grinned and let go of me, then left us to find himself a new willing dance partner.

I smiled up at my new husband as he crossed an arm in front of himself and dipped into a low bow before extending his hand out for me to take. I slipped my hand into his larger one and he pulled me into his embrace, then I followed his lead as he twirled me around the floor, keeping an easy pace with the lively pipes and bodran drums.

"Well, then, wife, are ye having a fine time?" he asked me.

"I am, husband. Thank you," I told him. I broke out into an unmanageable grin.

"There's no going back now, Glenna. You're well and truly mine."

"I thought I was already yours. Did you not believe that I meant to stay with you, then, even after everything? Maybe you expected me to slip out in the middle of the night, having changed my mind?" I teased him.

He raised an eyebrow at me and frowned slightly. "Aye, well, it surely wouldn't have been the first time, now, would it? I'm not ashamed to say I considered sleeping outside your door last night to make sure that I could catch ye in case ye decided to make a run for it."

"I'm glad you decided to trust me instead. That could have made for an awkward conversation with Anna in the morning when she came to help me get dressed."

"Do ye think she would have believed me if I told her I was there due to sleepwalking?" he asked me with a grin.

"I think she would have thought you a terrible liar, but would have been too polite to tell you so," I laughed.

Alastair pulled me tightly to him and kissed me

swiftly on the lips. I pulled away from him, my face burning as I heard the hollers of the revelers around us cheering at the sight.

"I look forward to being able to do that much more often. In fact, whenever the mood strikes me from now on," he said, grinning at me mischievously. Then he lowered his head to my shoulder and placed a soft kiss there before whispering softly in my ear, "There is one other thing I look forward to having the opportunity to do with you whenever the mood strikes."

My face flushed at the suggestiveness of his tone and I squirmed slightly as his fingers caressed my spine. He straightened slowly and looked me in the eye, his gaze unwavering, before looking away over the top of my head with a quick glance around the room. I followed him as he tugged on my hand and moved us quickly through the crowd as subtly as possible. We were stopped a few times by well-wishers but it didn't take us very long to make our way across the great hall in order to slip out the door as subtly as possible.

Once we were through the large doors and into the main hallway I gathered up the skirts of my gown and we took off for the staircase at a run. We did not stop once we hit the stairs, but hurried up to the floor of our bedchambers. We passed by my bedchamber door without a glance and moved toward Alastair's. The closer we got, the harder my heart began to hammer.

Alastair reached out and opened the door to his room and I hesitated before stepping inside. I could feel every inch of my body crying out for his and yet a part of me was still unbelievably nervous.

The room was cast in shadow, moonlight streaming in through the open window as I moved slowly toward the bed.

Alastair came up behind me and put his hands on my waist, pulling me back against him. Even through the layers of my wedding gown I could feel his readiness and my heartbeat quickened.

His hands slid up my sides to my shoulders and brushed my hair away from my neck so he could place a kiss there. I shuddered at the feather-light touch and closed my eyes to savor the moment.

"Ye look beautiful in the moonlight," he whispered.

I smiled and turned around to face him, reaching up to caress his face.

"You make me feel beautiful," I said, leaning in to him and tilting my head back.

Alastair lowered his face to mine and kissed me gently, teasing my lips with his. It felt wonderful, but I wanted more. A fire was beginning to burn inside of me and I kissed him back more forcefully, urging him on.

He walked me backwards until I felt the backs of my legs bump up against the bed. Very carefully, he helped me out of my gown, then let the soft, rich fabric pool on the floor.

My shift was soon to follow, and before I knew it I was standing in front of him completely naked.

A breeze blew through the room from the open window and I shuddered at the caress of the cool night air. My nipples puckered in the chill and Alastair reached out to me, ran his hands down my arms to grab my buttocks and lifted me up. I wrapped my legs around his waist and let my head fall back as his head dipped to feast first on one breast and then the other. The heat of his mouth clashed with the cool air in the room and my head spun from the intoxicating mix of temperatures and the wine I had drunk at the celebration.

Suddenly, I was slowly falling backwards and the softness of the bed came up to meet me even as I was covered by the weight of Alastair's body.

I ran my hands over the breadth of his back, then grabbed fistfuls of his shirt and tugged it up so that I could feel his skin.

Alastair sat up quickly and tugged the shirt over his head, then threw it aside. I tugged at his plaid, unwrapping his kilt, eager to have him as naked as I was. It was thrilling to know that this time we wouldn't have to stop. We were man and wife, and we could finally be together completely.

Alastair's hand tangled in my hair as we kissed. His mouth trailed down over my throat to my breast and then down over my stomach.

I gasped as his mouth covered the heat of me and my back arched as I felt his tongue probing at my core.

My fingers slipped through his hair as waves of pleasure crashed through my body.

I wanted to touch him, feel him, make him feel what I was feeling, but I could barely breathe, let alone think.

I felt like I was spiraling higher and higher. My entire body felt as if it were a spring, wound too tight and about to snap under the pressure. My legs began to shake as Alastair continued to pleasure me until finally I could not contain myself any longer. My body arched like a bow and I cried out at the top of my lungs, shouting my pleasure into the night.

Suddenly Alastair was above me, kissing me as he settled himself between my legs. I opened my legs wider to accommodate him and gasped at the pressure of his hardness probing against my entrance. My body stretched to fit him, and suddenly he was inside me. I cried out and bit his shoulder as he began to move slowly inside of me.

I felt as though I were floating and my hips came up to meet his as we picked up speed. My pleasure started to crest once more and my thigh muscles shook as we drove each other closer to the edge. Alastair's mouth covered mine as he roared his pleasure, the pumping of his hips forcing me to join him in our own private bliss.

I cried out once more as I threw myself over the edge into the waiting abyss with only the weight of Alastair's body to keep me anchored.

Afterward, we fell into a deep sleep, content and safe in each other's arms.

CHAPTER 26

"*A*lastair, please, you need to rest. You have been working all morning and you've yet to stop for a single bite to eat. You'll make yourself sick if you keep on this way." I stood just inside the doorway of Alastair's study and watched him as he pored over the correspondences that had arrived for him from the men that he had sent out to the neighboring clan lands.

"I'll stop to eat in a bit, lass. Don't fash yourself," he mumbled absently without looking up from the paper he was reading intently.

I shifted the tray in my hand and walked over to set it down on the edge of the desk, making sure to avoid putting it down on top of any of the papers he had scattered around him. The desk in his study looked as if a storm had been through it, wreaking a careless havoc as it tossed around everything in sight.

"Please, Alastair, you must eat. Just a bite," I pleaded with him. I rested my hand lightly on his shoulder before brushing back a thick lock of fire-red hair that had come loose from his plait.

He took hold of my hand and brought it to his lips to kiss the back of it before releasing it and sitting back heavily in his chair. He dropped the piece of correspondence he had been reading carelessly on top of all the others.

"Every one of them the same," he said with a snort of disgust. "Not a one of them has heard anything of use. Whoever these people are, they have covered their tracks disturbingly well, love."

"I refuse to believe that that our lack of information comes from any great skill on their end. It is more likely that they are able to stay hidden due to an overwhelming desire for self-preservation," I said, sniffing delicately. "Allina knows all of our strengths, all of our weaknesses. She would be sure to convey to whomever it is she has roped into helping her that they must observe the utmost caution in their actions. She knows how quickly you will move to destroy this threat the moment you discover where it is coming from. She would have to be prepared to move slowly and carefully so that she does not tip her hand too quickly and have us bring the battle to her doorstep."

"But to hear nothing, Glenna? Not so much as a whisper? How is that possible now that they know what we are?" Alastair slammed the flat of his hand down on his desk in frustration and I covered it with my own.

"Truth be told, I don't believe that she would be so foolish as to run through the highlands screaming of curses. She is too cunning. Your reputation lends itself to so much superstition that it would draw too much attention. But this, this slow quiet attack? The waiting, the uncertainty? It does its own damage and allows her to bide her time." I took his face in my hands and turned his head so that he looked at me straight on. "But it also gives us time, my love. It gives us time to prepare. When she makes her move we will be ready for her. We will not be caught unaware. And we will continue to search for her and root her out. She and whoever she found foolish enough to join her in this folly."

Alastair's eyes searched mine, then slowly, he reached out and slowly caressed my cheek. "Whatever would I do without ye, lass?" he asked me.

"Aren't you glad you'll never have to find out?" I said with a smile.

"Aye, I am."

"Come away with me," I pleaded with him. "Just for a short while. We can go for a walk, or a ride. The fresh air would do you some good. If you'll not eat, at least take a few minutes to stretch your legs. Please, Alastair. You've been in here for so long staring at these papers.

I'm amazed the words have not simply begun to blend together into an undecipherable mess."

"I canna, Glenna. There's too much work to be done." He shook his head and reached for one of the many papers on his desk.

"Alastair, you will drive yourself mad in here if you keep going on this way. Ever since that day in Fortingall you've done nothing but bury your head in these papers."

"I am sorry if I've not been sufficiently entertaining for you, lass, but believe it or not the future of my people if more important than your boredom."

I inhaled sharply and resisted the urge to smack him. "How dare you," I said quietly, my voice dripping with ice. "You think that I'm in here because I'm *bored*? Do you really think me so frivolous?" I grabbed the tray I had brought in with me, which carried what was to be his lunch, and picked it up off the desk roughly. The movement jostled the wine in the glass and some of the deep red liquid sloshed over the edge and onto the tray. "Fine. Sit here poring over your pages. Do you expect the words on the paper to magically change? That you will force them to reveal some new information by your sheer will? That would be quite the feat. Please, be sure to come find me when you do so that I can show you how properly impressed I am. And while you're working on that, you can continue to starve yourself as you seem so intent on doing," I snapped at him before turning for the door.

"Glenna, wait."

"No, no, I do not think I will," I said dismissively and kept walking.

"Glenna, I'm sorry. That was unkind of me," he said.

I could hear him standing up from his desk and I stopped my march toward the study door but I did not turn around. He came up behind me and placed both of his hands on my shoulders and I tensed in anger.

"Please, lass, I'm sorry. I never should have said such a thing to ye."

I forced the tension out of my shoulders and tried to let go of my anger. "I know how deeply the things you heard them saying in the village affected you," I said quietly. "And I know that you will feel the need to do everything in your power to prove to them that none of it was true. That they are right to put their faith in you. But you also need a clear head and to keep your body strong, otherwise you will be of no good to anyone."

He turned me around and I looked up into his face, which was clouded with contrition.

"You're right. I'll be of no use if I drive myself into the ground." He reached out to the tray and picked up the sandwich I had made for him. Smiling widely, he opened his mouth and took a huge bite and swallowed before taking another and then a third.

I stood waiting quietly while he finished his meal. I laughed as he winked at me then tipped his head back and emptied his glass of wine in a few gulps.

"Thank you," I said when he set the glass down on the tray beside the now empty plate.

"Nay, Glenna, thank ye." He leaned in and kissed me lightly at first and then after a moment began to kiss me more eagerly.

I sighed and started to lean into the kiss just as a knock came at the study door.

"Are we forever to be interrupted in this room?" he asked with a sigh as he pulled away and reached around me to open the door.

"My lord, my lady," said Gregory hastily as he tipped his head in my direction. "You must come quickly."

"What is it, Gregory?" I asked him.

Gregory looked back and forth between Alastair and me before he said, "The MacGregor has been challenged."

As we hurried to the great hall, a feeling of dread settled within me. To have someone step forward and challenge Alastair meant that he was starting to lose the trust of his people.

The room was already crowded when we arrived. Somehow word of the challenge must have spread throughout the castle. The crowd parted before us as we walked to the center of the room. The long table and benches had already been moved to the sides of the room, up against the walls.

I stood on the edge of the crowd as Alastair walked to the center of the large circle that had formed in the middle of the room. He turned, taking in the large group of clansmen who stood around him. I gritted my teeth at the sight of the fire that flashed in his haunting green eyes. It wasn't just anger that I saw there, but the ghost of betrayal. I did not pity the fool who had come to challenge my husband that day, but I held my breath and waited as he stood quietly waiting for the challenger to come forward.

There was a shuffling beside me as the people moved to let someone pass through, and I turned to look up into the face of the man we had seen in the town square in Fortingall just a week before. My eyes opened wide as he looked down at me for a moment with a determined expression on his face before he stepped forward to face Alastair.

"I've come to challenge the MacGregor!" His voice rang out loud and true around the room and reverberated off of the ceiling.

The room went dead silent at his announcement. It was one thing to hear that the MacGregor was to be challenged, and another thing completely to actually hear the challenge issued with your own ears. It felt as though everyone in the room took a communal step backward in an attempt to distance themselves from the man who had just spoken.

I worried my bottom lip, biting down on it painfully as I waited for Alastair's reply. The two men looked like giants as they stood facing one another.

Alastair took a step closer to his challenger and looked him over slowly from the ground up. "Ye think to challenge me for the position of chief of this clan?" he asked. Even though his voice was low, he was easily heard throughout the room.

"I challenge ye as leader of this pack. You've failed your people, Alastair MacGregor, by allowing the curse of the wolf to be known outside of McGregor lands. You've brought the enemy to our doorstep and some say behind these very walls. Ye have no business being Alpha."

"And ye think that you're the right wolf for the job, then, do ye?" Alastair growled.

"Aye, I do."

"Fine then, pup. I accept your challenge," said Alastair.

Graham bristled at being called pup then ignored it. "As our chief, you have the right to choose the time and place of the challenge."

"Tomorrow night at moonrise. There is a clearing not far from here. We will meet there," said Alastair decisively. His voice was cool and businesslike but I knew that the blood had to be boiling in his veins.

Graham bowed low and stayed doubled over until Alastair had walked away from him and exited the circle. He walked past me and headed straight for the door without stopping to look back. I turned to look at Graham and saw that he was also watching Alastair's departure with a strange look in his eye. His gaze slid to mine and our eyes locked. My jaw clenched in anger I turned my back on him, dismissing him sharply as I followed Alastair out the door.

CHAPTER 27

I stood like a statue and looked out the window, watching as the sky turned from blue to orange and pink as the sun began to set. I tried to calm the rapid beating of my heart but the slow deep breaths that I forced myself to take were of no use. I wouldn't have to wait much longer. In a few short minutes I, along with the rest of the castle's inhabitants, would exit out the castle doors and head into the woods toward the clearing where the challenge was to take place.

I clasped my hands together and brought them to my lips. Since the change I had gotten used to feeling warmer than I used to, but that evening my hands felt like blocks of ice, as though nothing in the world could warm them.

After the challenge had been issued Alastair had locked himself away and I hadn't seen him since. For the first time since I'd met him he had barred the door to the study, effectively locking me out, cutting me off from him. I felt completely helpless and utterly useless.

I held my hand up in front of my face and remembered the feel of the smooth wood of the study door beneath my fingertips. The door might as well have been made from iron, so efficient was it in barring my path. The only person to step foot past that door had been Alastair's uncle Donald. I could only hope that he had been able to offer my husband some sort of comfort and clarity.

The sun dipped lower toward the horizon and I left the room to head to the study. Just as I reached the door it opened and Alastair and Donald emerged. Donald looked tired but determined. He patted Alastair firmly on the back and gave his arm a quick squeeze.

"E'en Do bait Spair Nocht," he said to Alastair.

In what you do spare nothing. The MacGregor motto. There was no advice Alastair could have been given that would have been more fitting at that moment. No matter what was to come, Alastair could not afford to show any weakness.

Alastair turned his head in my direction and his eyes locked onto mine. They were shining brightly, with a wild look to them. I stepped forward, reaching out, and he pulled me to him, embracing me tightly.

"No matter what happens, know that I love you. If anything happens to me, I have made sure that Donald will ensure ye are well taken care of," he whispered into my hair.

"Do not say that," I hissed and jerked back. "Don't you dare say that. I will not stand here and listen to you say your goodbyes. Do you hear me? I will not stand for it, Alastair, I will not!" I was shouting by the end as I wrenched my way out of his arms.

"Glenna, nothing is certain, and we must be prepared…"

"No! I will not allow it. This will be over before it has begun. You are their rightful chief. You are their Alpha. You *will* prove that to every man, woman and child who bear the name MacGregor. And once this ridiculous challenge is finished and you have trounced that… that *mutt* into the dirt, we will go out and find Allina and drag her out of her hiding place by her hair and make her rue the day that she decided to start this trouble!"

The two men stood staring at me in silence, their mouths agape, as if I had just sprouted a second head. Suddenly Alastair threw back his head and roared with laughter.

"Ah, my little warrior. You've always a way of knowing exactly what I need even when I've not got a clue, haven't ye?"

I crossed my arms in front of my chest and sniffed dismissively. "We're going to be late," I told him and turned away.

I blinked rapidly in an attempt to hold back the

tears that threatened to surface and squared my shoulders. Alastair took my hand and jerked me back around to face him. His mouth crashed down onto mine and I accepted him eagerly. My fingers dug into the muscles of his arms as I clung to him fiercely. Although I refused to give voice to my fears, my body betrayed me as it trembled softly. Finally I took a deep breath and exhaled slowly, resting my forehead against his chest, soaking in the feel and scent of him.

"Come now, lass," he said to me quietly. "We must go."

I nodded silently and entwined my fingers with his. We walked as a group out of the castle and toward the open patch of glen where Alastair would fight to keep control of the clan and his pack.

The soft light of the setting sun filtered down through the shimmering leaves as the large group from the castle walked silently through the woods. Alastair and I led dozens of castle inhabitants to the challenge spot. Even though so many of us were moving though the trees, there was almost no sound as we stepped lightly through the underbrush.

Even the normal sounds of wildlife were silenced as we passed, as if the forest-dwelling animals knew what was about to happen. I could not hear a single birdsong, even with my new heightened hearing.

When we got to the clearing a large crowd of clansman had already gathered there. They stood behind Graham McConnell, whispering eagerly at the sight of our approach.

My heart sank at the sight of the group. It did not bode well that Graham had drawn so many people to his cause. I gritted my teeth in anger at the sight. Alastair had led and protected his clan for years. To see how quickly so many were able to turn their backs on him out of fear made my blood boil. The Clan McGregor had gone unchallenged for so long that they were letting their fear cloud their judgment at the first sign of trouble.

How could they hold their heads high and call themselves wolves when they showed such cowardice and disloyalty?

As we came up to the edge of the challenge area, the groups on either side spread out to flank the two men, wrapping around the open space in a circle, effectively closing them in. In the center of the circle stood the magistrate, Mr. Alpin. His face bore a grim expression and his eyes betrayed his fatigue with deep lines etched into the soft, plump skin near his eyes.

We stood silently and waited with bated breath as the last few rays of daylight began to disappear and Mr. MacAlpin slowly raised his hands above his head, the flats of his palms turned out in front of him as though he were trying to hold back the tide.

"We come together on this night to bear witness to

the challenge called forth by our clansman Graham McConnell. Graham has challenged our chief Alastair MacGregor for the right to lead our people as Alpha of our pack."

The people around me shifted uncomfortably and I scanned the crowd to take in their reactions to the words being spoken.

Mr. MacAlpin lowered his left hand and held it out toward Alastair, who nodded and stepped forward into the clearing. Once Alastair had reached the magistrate, Mr. MacAlpin lowered his right hand out to Mr. McConnell, who stepped forward silently to join the other two men. Then the magistrate took a deep, shaky breath and pulled himself up to his full height, which was still well below the shoulders of the two larger men who flanked him, facing each other.

I searched Graham's face, but it betrayed no emotion.

Mr. MacAlpin reached up and placed a hand on each man's shoulder, then stepped back out of the way until he found a place at the edge of the ring among the crowd.

The moment the area was clear, Graham swung his fist directly at Alastair's face. The movement was so sudden that I gasped, my hands flying to my mouth as Alastair bent back at the waist, just barely dodging the blow.

Graham stepped forward to close the distance, throwing a punch with his other hand, but Alastair ducked beneath it, stepping forward to meet Graham and bringing his own fist up to connect with the bottom of Graham's jaw. My eyes went wide as Graham's head snapped back from the force of the blow before he doubled over, Alastair's fist now planted firmly in the pit of his stomach.

Before Alastair had a chance to strike again, Graham shoved him back with both hands, slammed palms-first into Alastair's chest. Having put some distance between them, Graham had a moment to collect himself and prepare for Alastair's next attack. The men moved around each other smoothly, each taking the other man's measure before stepping in and striking out.

As the fighting went on, the blows got harder and less forgiving, each man throwing his entire weight behind his blow, determined to bring his opponent to his knees.

Suddenly, I heard Alastair roar in pain and saw him stumble back from Graham's outstretched arm. He turned toward me to reveal the ragged tears in his shirt, the edges soaked in blood and the long gashes in the flesh beneath.

The fingers on Graham's hand were elongated into vicious-looking claws and rage welled up in me at the sight.

"Foul!" I screamed, lunging forward. I didn't know if partial transformations were against the rules of the challenge or not, but I didn't care. This whole challenge seemed wrong to me.

Donald's arms wrapped tightly around my waist and he hauled me backward off my feet before I had been able to take two steps toward the fighters.

"Hold, lass! Ye canna interfere in this," he hissed in my ear.

I struggled against him for a moment before taking a deep breath and nodding in acceptance. Once Donald was sure that I had my emotions under control, he eased his grip on me and then let me go.

Alastair tore away the tattered remains of his shirt, exposing the injury for all to see. I watched as the muscles began to swell and roll beneath his skin and I took an involuntary step back as he began to shift.

Graham wasted no time in quickly pulling off his own shirt so he could shift completely as well, and soon two giant wolves stood in the clearing where the two men had been.

I watched as the pitch-black wolf that was Alastair circled around the honey-brown wolf that was Graham with his head low and his lips pulled back in a deep snarl.

Graham snapped his jaws at him and the two wolves lunged for each other, tearing at fur and flesh with their claws and teeth as they fought for purchase and the upper hand.

Graham's jaws closed around Alastair's shoulder and clamped down, causing Alastair to howl in pain.

My hand flew to Donald's and squeezed his fingers in fear. Donald pulled me closer to him so that we stood side by side, our arms pressed against each other and our fingers tightly entwined as we watched the two wolves roll over on top of one another in the grass.

Graham had Alastair pinned beneath him and had started to lower his jaws to the back of Alastair's neck when Alastair turned and threw Graham off at the last moment. Taking advantage of his moment of freedom, Alastair dove for Graham and wasted no time in wrapping his jaw around Graham's neck and squeezing.

I squeezed my eyes shut against the sound of Graham's pained howls, but forced myself to open them again at Donald's jostling against me. I had to watch to the very end. I listened to Alastair's enraged snarls as he shook Graham, and I waited, on edge, to hear the inevitable snap of Graham's neck breaking, but it never came.

Surprisingly, Alastair stopped shaking his head and Graham lay still, trapped between his jaws, whimpering softly. I watched in shock as Alastair released the other wolf and took a step back from his opponent. Graham continued to lie there as Alastair shifted back to human form and bent down to wrap his plaid around his waist, covering his nudity.

He looked down at Graham and then around at the faces staring at him in open-mouthed confusion. "I am your chief and your Alpha, by blood and by deed!" he roared. "I have been challenged and yet I stand before ye bloodied but unbested. If any of ye still doubt the right of my claim, step forward now and claim your right of challenge. But I warn ye, ye will fare no better than the wolf ye see here before ye." He pointed down to Graham, then walked over to where the other man's plaid lay in the dirt and draped it carefully over the wolf's body.

"We are one clan. One blood. One spirit! I know that ye are afraid. Never before have we faced such attack. But we are MacGregors! We are wolf born! We will face our opponents and we shall show them no fear. We shall show them nothing but the flash of claw and the glint of fang before we send them to meet their Creator. I ask ye to stand by me! To trust in me! And to fight by my side, because together we shall show all just what it means to carry the name MacGregor!"

The clearing erupted into cheers and whistles of support at his speech.

Alastair bent down and extended his hand to Graham, who had shifted back to human form. Graham clutched his plaid around him as he took Alastair's hand and was pulled gingerly to his feet. Alastair stepped forward and embraced Graham gently, mindful of his wounds, before stepping back and holding Graham's hand high in the air.

The crowed cheered even louder and I let out a sigh of relief. Alastair's position with the clan was secure once more, but I had no doubt in my mind that our work had only just begun.

CHAPTER 28

*B*ack in our bedchamber I watched in tense silence as the housekeeper, Mrs. Fletcher, saw to Alastair's wounds. He sat stripped to the waist, offering me a clear view of the deep, angry gashes across his chest where Graham had slashed him. The wounds had already begun to close, but I knew that I would not be able to breathe easily again until the flesh was once again smooth and unmarked.

Graham had been brought with us back to the keep and as soon as Mrs. Fletcher had seen to her chief's wounds she would leave to see to those of the defeated challenger. Even though I was against it, I had bitten my tongue in the clearing when Alastair had commanded Donald to help Graham back to the castle with us so that he could be seen to. It worried me to think that the man who would have killed Alastair less than one short hour ago was now going to be sleeping under our roof.

"You're a tough lad, Alastair. Your father would have been proud of ye today," said Mrs. Fletcher as she packed up the bloody cloths and the red-tinged bowl of water that she had been using to clean Alastair's wounds.

"Thank ye, Mrs. Fletcher. It's kind of ye to say so," said my husband, squeezing her hand gently.

"'Tis no kindness on my part but the simple truth. We are in troubled times, young MacGregor, but this evening ye carried yourself with honor and showed mercy where you needn't have. He lost his challenge and in doing so his death was your due, and yet ye spared him his life. You've a good heart in ye, even at the most trying of times. Your father would be proud to see that."

Mrs. Fletcher squeezed his shoulder and nodded silently to me before letting herself quietly out of the chamber.

Once she had left Alastair stood and barred the door behind her before walking over to the side table to poor himself some wine.

"Here," I said, standing quickly and taking the pitcher from him. "Let me do that. You go sit down."

"There's no need to fuss over me, Glenna. I'll be fine," he protested, but he released his grip on the jug and allowed me to pour.

"Well, you may not need it, but maybe I do. Maybe I need to fuss over you a bit," I said softly.

The candle flames flickered in the light breeze from the open window, throwing our shadows dancing across the walls. I watched them absently for a moment, focusing on them so that my mind wouldn't wander back to the fight in the forest.

"For a moment there I thought that I might lose you," I admitted, turning around to hand him the glass of wine.

The corner of his mouth turned up in a wry smile and he moved stiffly to sit on the edge of the bed before taking a deep swallow from his cup. "Did ye think that my time had come?" he asked with a hint of laughter in his voice.

"No, I just…" I trailed off before beginning again. "There was one moment when he had you pinned and I saw him about to bite the back of your neck. I don't believe that I've ever been so afraid before in my life. You let him live, once you knew that you had won, but I don't believe that he would have done the same for you."

I shook my head and began to pace as the words tumbled out of me. "If Mr. McConnell had succeeded in defeating you, I am certain that he would have taken your life. I would be here, a widow, my heart broken and mourning you. And yet he is here under our roof. His wounds are being dressed at this very moment. I find it hard to believe that it is just... over as easily is that. I do not trust him. How can you trust him?"

"He is of clan MacGregor."

"But he challenged you!" I insisted.

"And if not him it would have been another. The people are scared. They needed a show of strength. I needed to be reminded that I could lead them, defend them. Any member of this clan has the right to challenge for the position to lead."

"But what if someone else tries to challenge you now? Or what if he tries again? Or tries something underhanded next time?"

"Graham McConnell would never be able to assume lead of this clan if he were to get rid of me through an underhanded deed. If I die before you bear me a son, then command would fall to my uncle Donald. The only chance Graham had of taking command from me was in the woods tonight. He had no reason to believe that he would come out of that challenge alive if he were to lose. I do not think that he would be so foolish as to throw his life away now by trying to make another move against me. What he did, I'm sure he did for what he believed to be the good of the clan."

"I don't know how you can be so calm about this, have such faith in his intentions," I grumbled.

"I am their chief. I must stay calm and clear-headed. And I know my people. I have to believe in them, otherwise we have already lost. If we are not fighting for each other, then what are we fighting for?"

I shook my head and crossed my arms over my chest. "So are you telling me that you would now have this man fighting at your side? You would trust him to watch your back in battle after this? You would put your life in his hands?" I asked in disbelief.

"I will give him the opportunity to prove himself, yes. We must show a united front, Glenna, and the only way to do that is with trust. And to trust someone is always taking a risk."

I sighed heavily and covered my face with my hands before dropping them back down to my sides in frustration. "I do not know how you do it," I said finally. "How you walk such a line every day."

"Come sit with me," he said, patting the bed beside him. "I want to tell you about my father."

I sat down next to Alastair, careful not to brush up against him. He was bruised and torn beneath the bandages wrapped around his forearm where Graham had gotten his teeth into him. Alastair might have been willing to put his trust in Graham and his intentions, but I was not.

He took my hand in his, mindless of his injured arm, and pulled it over to rest on his knee. "My father was the strongest man I have ever known. Not just physically, but mentally as well. From the day I was born he raised me to lead this clan. To always put the needs of my people before my own. That in and of itself was nay less than what any chief should be raised to do, but there was always an extra edge to my father's teachings. He didn't just want me to be a good man, but to be a great man. From as early as I can remember he pressed upon me the importance of protecting my people from those who would not understand what we were."

"It's a great responsibility," I whispered.

He nodded and looked off into the flame of a nearby candle. His eyes were distant as he thought back to the past. "As far back as I can remember, my father was there, teaching and guiding me."

"What happened to your parents?" I asked. My heart felt as if an iron band had been wrapped tightly around it.

"They died together," he said, his voice tight with emotion. "We were out running together one night and were separated. While we were apart, they were attacked by a sick wolf, one whose mind had obviously snapped from the stress of the change. The wolf attacked my mother and cornered her at the edge of a cliff. She was a brave woman, and she held her own. My father went to protect her and dove for the other wolf. The three of them tangled together as my parents tried to take the wolf down, but suddenly they were falling, and they all went over the cliff together. I found them too late, and was too far away to stop any of it from happening, it all happened so fast. By the time I reached the edge of the cliff, it was too late."

Alastair closed his eyes and shook his head. "There are many injuries that we can survive, but the fall was just too much. Maybe if they fell individually? Maybe if they were not so injured before the fall? I canna say, and there is no going back and changing it now."

"I'm so sorry for your loss, my love. I wish that I could have met them."

"They would have loved ye, Glenna, of that I'm sure. They would have thought ye very kind and very brave. They would have been proud to have ye as their daughter."

I hastily wiped a tear away from my eye and gave him a watery smile. "I would have been proud to know them as well. I would have loved to have met the people who raised such an amazing man, if only to thank them for making my happiness possible." I leaned forward and kissed him softly, mindful of his split lip. "Your parents would be so very proud of the man you have become."

"Thank ye, love. I truly hope so."

CHAPTER 29

I knocked on the door to Alastair's study and walked in carrying a tray of cups, a large jug of ale and a hearty lunch of cold meats and bread. He had been in there all morning with Donald, Gregory and Mr. MacAlpin, poring over the latest correspondences from the scouts he had sent out. They had been so focused on working on a strategy that they had not stopped to eat for hours.

When I stepped into the room I stopped short, surprised by the sight of Graham McConnell sitting with the other men in the chairs around the large desk. I moved forward slowly, trying to organize my thoughts as my mind reeled. Why would Alastair let this man take part in this?

My eyes never left his back as I made my way forward, trying desperately to resist the urge to throw one of the cups I was carrying at the back of his head.

He must have sensed my eyes on him because he suddenly turned and I found myself trapped in his piercing gaze. He cocked an eyebrow at me and stared back for a moment before one corner of his mouth turned up in a slight smile before settling again, as if he could read my thoughts.

I narrowed my eyes at him and tore my gaze away from his, only for it to land on Alastair, who was looking at me quizzically. I set the tray down on the desk with a little more force than I had intended and paused for a moment, hoping that no one had noticed.

"Is that tray a little heavy there, lass?" Donald asked me.

"I suppose it was a bit heavier than I thought it would be," I said, avoiding his gaze.

We all knew that now that I had the wolf in me, the tray was feather light, but I refused to rise to his teasing. I wanted to get out of the room as quickly as possible before I let my temper get the better of me. Pardoning Graham for challenging him was one thing, but Alastair was taking things a bit far.

I could feel Graham's eyes on me but I refused to look his way. I would not give him the satisfaction of seeing me so uncomfortable.

"I'll just leave you all to your planning," I said as calmly as possible and strode from the room, closing the door firmly behind me, all the while resisting the urge to slam it so hard the walls shook.

"Glenna?"

I tensed at the sound of Graham's voice and my hands clenched into tight fists at my sides before I took a deep breath and turned around to face him. My toe tapped impatiently on the damp grass as I waited for him to cross the last bit of distance between us.

"Good afternoon, Mr. McConnell. Are you all finished for the day?" I asked as politely as possible.

"No, I will be going back inside shortly, but the MacGregor thought that we should break for a few minutes to clear our heads."

"Oh, well, please, don't let me disturb you," I said with a slight incline of my head before turning to depart.

"Please," he said, taking a step toward me.

I took a hasty step back before crossing my arms over my chest and standing my ground. "Yes?" I asked, snapping out the word.

"I had hoped to speak to ye, if ye have a few minutes to spare."

He took another step toward me, but this time I didn't retreat. I tilted my head back and raised myself to my full height.

I had never known another man as large as Alastair, but Graham came unnervingly close.

"What..." My voice wavered, so I cleared my throat

and started again. "What would you like to speak to me about?"

"I know that ye don't trust me, but I mean ye no harm."

I snorted softly and rolled my eyes at him. "If you mean me no harm, you have a strange way of showing it."

He frowned at me and crossed his own arms, mirroring my stance. "Have I harmed ye in any way?" he asked.

"You mean other than trying to kill my husband?" I snapped, rapidly losing my temper.

"I had no intention of killing your husband, Lady MacGregor."

"I find that rather hard to believe. Wasn't that you with your jaws wrapped around my husband's neck? Do you expect me to believe that you would have spared his life if he had not won your fight?"

He opened his mouth to answer, then closed it again, saying nothing.

"I didn't think so," I said with a glare.

"Your husband is the chief and Alpha of our pack. He is leader of our clan and I respect that."

I looked at him in confusion, confounded by the words coming out of his mouth. "Have you lost your mind? Are you insane? For surely you must be if you expect me to believe something so blatantly untrue. One minute you try to usurp his position and the next you claim to respect him and the title that he holds? Words have never before rung so false in my ears! You insult me, sir, with your obvious assumption that I am so feebleminded that I could be swayed by such empty words!"

"And your husband, my lady, is he feebleminded too then?" Graham countered. "For ye saw yourself this very day the trust that he has in me. Why else would he allow me into his counsel? Why would he let me be witness to the plans to be set forth?"

"My husband is no fool. While I cannot claim to understand the reasoning behind his actions as of yet, I have every faith that he sees you for the lying, deceitful snake that you are. He is wise to keep his enemies close, very wise indeed. And you will never be able to convince me that you are anything but a danger to him."

"I know that I will have to work to gain your trust, Lady MacGregor."

I held up my hand to silence him and shook my head firmly. "Keep your words, for they hold less substance than the breath in which you speak them. I tell you this now, Graham McConnell—there is nothing that you could do in this life or the next that could convince me that you mean us anything but harm. I will be watching you very closely, make no mistake about that."

I turned on my heels and stormed away, my temper

fuming. The gall of that man. Who did he think he was to believe that my mind could be swayed and my eyes blinded by a few pretty words of apology?

CHAPTER 30

"*A* rider comes, a rider!"

I looked up from the dough I was kneading in the kitchen. After a week of finding myself doing more than my share of pacing around the castle, I had decided the only thing for me to do was to put myself to work. I found the rough kneading and rolling of the bread dough to be nothing as I beat it into shape before setting it aside to rise.

I stepped away from the thick roll of dough as the words were repeated in hushed excitement around the kitchen.

"Who has come?" I asked one of the maids.

She started, unsure of herself now that she had been directly addressed. When I came down to the kitchens earlier, I had seen a few curious glances cast my way, but for the most part the maids kept to themselves and

I was more than happy to get on with my tasks in silence, with only Mrs. Fletcher for conversation.

"We don't know, m'lady, only that he rode so hard his horse near collapsed once it got to the gates. Whatever his reason for being here, the news must be very urgent."

I nodded to her and used my apron to hastily wipe the flour from my hands and arms before tossing it on the counter. "Excuse me Mrs. Fletcher, but I must go," I said to the housekeeper as I took off for the stairs that led out of the kitchen and up to the main level of the keep.

When I got upstairs I looked around, but although there was a buzz of excited voices I saw neither Donald nor Alastair around. I hurried quickly to the study. I was sure that the rider had already been taken there.

My heart hammered in my chest as I hurried through the halls. There was no doubt that whoever had arrived was one of the men Alastair had sent to find out about Allina's plans. Maybe we had finally had a stroke of good luck.

I knocked twice on the study door and rushed inside without waiting for an answer. Inside, Alastair, Donald, Gregory, and Graham were gathered around a slight, flaxen-haired clansman who was slumped in a chair, eagerly finishing glass after glass of water. In his rush, he spilled the liquid over the side of the glass and down the front of his shirt, but he did not slow, simply handed over the empty cup to be refilled once more.

"Thank ye, Lord MacGregor, sir," he said, short of breath once he had finished his glass of water.

"Just breathe, Malcolm, and take it slow. Catch your breath for a minute."

"No time," Malcolm said, shaking his head as he tried to push himself up straighter in the chair. He was too weak to support himself and collapsed backwards again.

"What have ye learned, Malcolm?" Donald asked. His forehead was furrowed in worry as he took in Malcolm's appearance.

"It's the Campbells," Malcolm panted. "She's enlisted the help of the Campbells. They'll be marching on us at any time now. I know not how many men they will send, but I can tell ye it will nay be a paltry few. They mean to wipe us out, my lord. Cleanse the earth of us and all of those with the curse."

"How did ye learn of this?" Gregory asked.

Malcolm shook his head and closed his eyes as he tried to get his breathing under control. I wanted to take the man by the shoulders and shake the answers out of him, but I resisted the urge and let him tell us in his own time.

"At first there was nothing. There was nary a whisper of knowledge of us, ye ken. It was so quiet for so long that I was starting to wonder if Allina had realized the folly of her ways and had decided to put all thoughts of vengeance out of her mind." He sighed heavily. Such a fool's dream.

"I travelled from pub to pub and kept an ear out for any rumors, dropping a hint here and there over a game or two of cards or dice. Get a man drunk enough and they'll gossip just as badly as any woman." He held his glass up and Alastair refilled it again. "And then one night my work paid off. I was sitting in the corner nursing a whiskey when I noticed a table of young men who looked to be around my age out of the corner of my eye. They were whispering in hushed but obviously eager voices. Their faces were flushed in the low light, but they glowed with something more than the warmth of good drink. And then I heard it, the name MacGregor. I tried to listen carefully but I could only pick out a few words. But what I did pick up on, clear as day, was that the MacGregors were finally going to get what was coming to them."

"And?" Gregory asked, eager for more. I too was leaning forward in anticipation of the rest of the story.

"Well, I figured the only way to find out what they had planned was to go join their group and drown the details out of them, so that's what I did. Turns out they were new recruits to the Campbells' new cause and were out celebrating being initiated into the ranks of hunters. It didn't take much to get them to loosen their tongues. Allina was able to get the ear of Robert Campbell. Seduced her way into his bed, most likely." Malcolm's eye caught mine and he cleared his throat, blushing. "Begging your pardon, my lady. I meant no offense."

"Of course," I said, waving away his worries. "Please continue."

"Well, from what I could make out, once she had his attention, she begged his assistance in clearing the highlands of the devil's scourge. She told him of our abilities and whatever she told him must have been all too convincing, because he started recruiting hunters to invade our lands and hunt us down."

"It probably didn't take all that much convincing on her part," I said absently. "The MacGregors have done a fine job of weaving a cloak of mystery and suspicion about themselves. People are eager to believe that you're in league with the devil, if you're not the very devil himself. And now one of your own has confirmed their deepest suspicions. What more could they need to begin gathering their courage? Suspicion is one thing, but her plea for help is tantamount to an outright confession."

"Exactly, my lady," Malcolm said with a nod. "Once I learned that the Campbells planned to march on our clan lands within the week, I rode as hard and as fast as possible. I did not stop for water or food, barely pausing to shut my eyes for a single hour at a time. I knew that we would need all the time possible to alert our people and prepare."

Alastair patted the man on the shoulder. "Thank ye, Malcolm. I'm grateful for all that you've done. You've given us a chance to protect our people."

"Alastair, we have to get word to everyone. Will we have enough time?" I asked.

"We have no choice but to try. I'll send out another group of riders to alert the people in every village and crofting."

"What of those people who have no wolf?" I asked. "Will they also be in danger?"

"Yes, lass, they will," said Donald gravely. "I doubt the Campbells are planning on knocking on each door and asking nicely which ones of us do and which ones dinna. They mean to kill as many of us as they can."

"But we'll not go without a fight," snarled Graham.

Alastair nodded in agreement. "All we have wanted is to be left in peace. To mind our lands and raise our families without interference. If the Campbells have decided it's war they want, then it's war they'll get."

"The Campbells are a huge clan. They could easily outnumber us" I said to the men.

"They are still only human," Gregory said confidently. "We have advance notice and can best them in strength as well as speed. They don't stand a chance."

I nodded in agreement but worried my bottom lip and wrapped my arms around myself. I was suddenly cold, as if a chill had passed through the room.

"We need to send men out right away," Donald told Alastair. "I'll get the riders organized and send them on their way."

"I'll ride into Fortingall with some men and round

up the people to tell them what we know," offered Graham.

I looked at him, remembering the sentiments he'd been telling the crowd the last time he had gathered the people in Fortingall's town square.

He looked back at me and smiled as if he could read my mind and knew exactly what I was thinking. "Don't worry, Lady MacGregor. I promise you I won't be saying anything that ye could find objectionable."

An unwanted smile started to tug at the corner of my mouth at his teasing but I narrowed my eyes at him instead, not wanting him to know that I had found his comment amusing. I had learned over the past few months that I was much too eager to trust and befriend people, and I was determined not to make that same mistake again. Especially when we already had one enemy nearly upon our doorstep, it was more important than ever to keep our eyes open for those that might already be inside our gates.

"Gregory," Alastair barked, "spread the word to the castle inhabitants to make their way to the great hall. They need to be told now. I'll expect everyone there within fifteen minutes. Ye all know what you're to be doing, so let's be quick about it."

We left the study as a group but slowly broke off in different directions to gather the men needed to spread the word to the far-reaching clansmen.

Even riding at top speed it would be slow work.

The men would have to stop at every home and tavern they could find in order to tell everyone about the impending invasion. By now word should have spread that there was a threat against the clan, but I doubted that the reality of the situation had really hit the MacGregors yet. They had lived in relative peace and secrecy for so long, how would they take the knowledge that not only was their secret out, but a clan easily thee times their size now planned on conquering and killing them? Wiping them out completely?

Gregory was convinced that we would win due to our speed and strength. But the percentage of the clan that actually had wolf blood was relatively small. What would happen to all of the people who didn't have the gift of heightened speed and strength? There were entire families without the ability to shift who had never had to defend themselves before.

No matter how badly I wanted to believe that we would be able to face the Campbells and win, I feared for the lives that would be lost in the war. People were about to die; there was simply no avoiding it.

My heart pounded so hard in my chest that I was sure Alastair could hear it as he walked beside me, but he said nothing, merely reached out and took my hand in his, giving it a reassuring squeeze before releasing it again and walking into the great hall.

As I looked around I suddenly saw the room covered in flowers and greenery. People spun and laughed as music cut through the air. The joy of our wedding seemed so long ago.

The image faded away and I looked around at the drawn, scared faces of our people.

People would die, that was unavoidable, but we would do everything in our power to make sure that we saved as many of them as we could.

CHAPTER 31

Tension could be felt in the air over the next few days as the MacGregors prepared for the Campbell invasion. Men were put on rotation around the castle and Fortingall, as well as stationed down the roads so that we could be warned as soon as the marching men came into sight.

The men gathered in the town square and the fields, practicing their swordsmanship. Every male old enough to fight had a weapon pressed into his hands. I worked with the women to gather clean rags for bandages so that we could see to the wounded. While those capable of shifting were also fast helpers, there were many people who would be in need of medical attention and I wanted to make sure that we were prepared to take care of them as quickly as possible. Mrs. Fletcher and I were run off our feet as we gathered all of the willow bark we could to boil into tea to soothe the pain of the injured.

I hurried through the town to the church, where we had set up the healing station. I nodded to the large guards posted in front of the doors as I passed through. They were twin brothers, only a few inches taller than I was, and stocky of build, with honey-blond hair. Although I had seen them around the keep time and again I had never had a chance to get to know them. But Ian and Liam were always quick with a smile, even now, and I was glad that they were the ones assigned to be our shadows while we were in town. The church was to be defended at all times. While we hoped that we would have adequate warning when the Campbells arrived, Alastair was not taking any chances. Once the fighting started we would be separated, Alastair to lead his men, and I to help with the caring for the wounded.

I looked back over my shoulder to see a group of women rushing toward the town square. I knew that those women capable of shifting had demanded to join the fighting. They would defend their homes, and the MacGregor had accepted their help without hesitation. The women were strong and capable; no one would deny that. One shifter woman would be able to handle any Campbell man who dared to attack her or those she loved.

I was sorry that I could not fight at Alastair's side. I wanted to fight with him, to defend my husband and my people as a newly turned wolf. All I could do was pray that those men he had with him would defend his life where I could not. When all of this was over, I wanted my husband standing by my side.

"Just set that lot down over there, Lady MacGregor, with the other," said Mrs. Fletcher as she wiped the perspiration from her forehead with the sleeve of her gown.

I set down the raw woven bag I was carrying and the cups inside clattered loudly against each other. "Do you think that will be enough cups?" I asked her, looking at the pile.

"It will have to do. I'm more worried about ensuring we've enough fresh water for both drinking and cleansing their wounds," she told me.

I nodded in understanding. If we ran out of water in the middle of the fighting, it would be very difficult to get some more. I had already ordered that five large barrels of it be transferred to the church so that we wouldn't be caught without it.

"And we've enough wood for the fire so that we can boil it?"

"Yes," she said, nodding. "And I've sent two of the girls out to gather some more. They should be back shortly."

"I hope that the other towns are using this time wisely to prepare. I hate the thought of them being caught unaware." I looked out the window to the pale blue sky. Afternoon was coming to an end and it wouldn't be long until we had to pack our things and head back to the castle.

Mrs. Fletcher came and stood beside me. After a moment she slid her hand into mine. Her skin was thin and papery, and even though I could feel the hard calluses she bore from a life of hard work, the skin on the back of her hand was still very soft.

"Our men will have ridden long and hard. They know what is at stake. They've been sure to tell the others what's needed if we're to survive this, Lady MacGregor. I've know doubt of that. Everyone will be preparing themselves, just the same as us. And when the Campbell men take their first foolish steps onto our land, they'll find themselves living their worst nightmares. Ye don't just walk into a wolf's woods as bold as ye please and expect to come out alive. They think we're devils and demons? We'll show them hell, no doubt about it."

I nodded and squeezed her hand. "You're a fine woman, Mrs. Fletcher, and I'm proud to be working alongside you in this."

"And I you, my lady. I'll not deny that when ye first came to us, I had my doubts," she said gruffly. "But I've come to see that you're just as much a MacGregor as the rest of us. The MacGregor couldn't have picked a finer woman as his wife."

"Thank you," I told her, touched by her admission.

"Come now," she said, pulling her hand from mine

so she could smooth the wrinkles on the front of her serviceable brown gown. "There's more to be doing around here and not nearly enough time to be doing it in."

I walked out of the church as the sun was beginning to set and was surprised to find Alastair waiting for me outside. He was sitting atop a large white horse and his hands held the reins of a second mount that I assumed was meant for me.

"What are you doing here?" I asked him.

He looked weary. Deep lines were etched into his face, and though he sat straight in the saddle, I could make out the effort it took him to keep his back rigid. He would not want to show any sign of weakness.

The two guards who had been sent to protect us were heading toward their horses with Mrs. Fletcher and the kitchen maids who had been assigned to us for medical duty. Alastair moved to dismount but I held up my hand to stop him. I was easily able to climb up onto my horse without any assistance.

"We were finished sooner than I expected, and I wanted to escort ye back to the keep. I'd like to spend as much time with ye as possible while we can," he said. As soon as I was seated he took my arm and tugged me sideways, then leaned closer to press a quick kiss to my lips, headless of those around us.

I pulled away to see Donald looking at us. When he saw that he had my attention, he wiggled his eyebrows at me and blinked boldly. I could feel my face growing warm as I blushed lightly. I loved when Alastair kissed me, but I sometimes felt self-conscious when he did it in front of others.

"Come on, lad, we canna be sitting around all here all night while you make calf eyes at your wife," Donald barked jokingly as he kicked his horse into a trot.

I dug my heels into my horse's flank and started off after him, laughing instinctively at the scowl Alastair leveled at his uncle's back. I was caught off-guard by the sound. I couldn't remember the last time I had heard laughter since we got word that the Campbells were soon to be on the move.

Alastair looked over at me and grinned widely. The strain of the day seemed to fall from his shoulders as he pulled his horse just ahead of mine and picked up speed. I urged my horse faster and faster, until its nose inched past the nose of Alastair's mount.

Tossing my hair back over my shoulder, I leaned forward in my saddle until Alastair was fully behind me. I looked back at him and laughed. Accepting my challenge, Alastair urged his horse faster to keep up with me and we continued to race out of Fortingall and down the road toward the castle, our horses staying neck and neck with one another.

Because they could not risk losing sight of us, the others joined our race, and soon our entire party was laughing as we galloped down the winding road, each of us trying to pull ahead of the other, enjoying for the moment the freedom from worry and doubt.

Suddenly, Ian jerked in his saddle and his horse stumbled. I watched as one hand went to his shoulder while he tried to gain control of his horse with the other. Even as he struggled, Ian's head was up, scanning the trees on either side of the road, his head whipping back and forth. When he turned in his saddle I saw a large arrow shaft sticking out of his shoulder and I too scanned the crowd for attackers.

Ian's brother was soon at his side, his sword drawn, ready for another attack, determined to defend his brother.

Ian took hold of the arrow shaft and pulled, wrenching if free from his shoulder just as a second arrow flew past, just barely missing Alastair.

"They are tipped in silver!" Ian yelled in warning.

"Spread out!" Alastair yelled. "Find them! Glenna, guard the women!"

I wheeled my horse around and herded Mrs. Fletcher and the girls into a tight circle. Whipping my head around, I took note of in which directions the men were headed into the trees.

My shock that Alastair would leave me to defend the other women by myself was quickly replaced with pride and then determination. This was what I had wanted: a chance to prove that I could be useful when the time came.

There was a rustling in the trees and I tensed, preparing myself to lunge from my horse and shift, but it was not needed. Alastair emerged from the trees, a struggling man bound tightly in his grip, cursing Alastair's name. When they reached the road Alastair held the man up in front of his chest and Liam pressed the point of his dirk to the man's throat.

"Ye shot my brother," he snarled at the man, pressing until a bright spot of blood welled up and the crimson bead rolled down his throat.

"I was trying to shoot the MacGregor," the prisoner snarled, "but I canna say I'm sorry that my arrow found a new target."

"How many more of ye are there?" Alastair demanded as Liam leaned in menacingly.

"I'll never tell ye, so you'll just have to kill me, and then you'll ever know, will ye? So ye might as well get on with it, then."

I could hear a low, menacing growl coming from Liam as he grabbed the man by the throat and shook him roughly. "How many!" he shouted.

"I'll not tell ye a thing!" The man spat in Liam's face and grinned triumphantly.

"Look away, Glenna," Alastair said quietly.

The simmering rage in his voice made the hair on the back of my neck stand up. I quickly turned away from the sight, directing the other women to do the same.

A loud crack rang out and the man's agonized

screams tore through the air. I risked glancing over my shoulder to see tears streaming down the man's face and his left arm hanging strangely. I had no doubt that the arm was broken and that he would have been doubled over in pain if it were not for Alastair holding him upright so that Liam could continue to question him.

"Now, I'll be asking ye for the last time. Are there any more men in the trees?"

"No," the Campbell man said, shaking his head. "There's no one but me. I was just meant to keep watch. But when I saw the MacGregor riding by, I thought I'd take my chance and rid the highlands of the devil spawn myself."

Alastair jerked him roughly and the man groaned in pain. "How far away are the rest of the Campbells?" Alastair demanded. "How many are coming for us?"

"As many as we could find." The man tried to laugh but he trailed off weakly, his bravado slipping away.

Alastair grabbed the man's injured arm and pulled on it and the man screamed again. His face went bone-white and his Adam's apple bobbed rhythmically, as if he were trying to keep himself from being sick.

"How many!" Alastair shouted.

"Hundreds," the man hissed. "Enough to wipe ye and your cursed filthy clan from the earth and send ye back to the hell from where ye came. We'll be upon ye before ye've blinked."

"We'll be sure to keep our eyes open, then," Alastair said calmly, with a nod to Liam.

Liam sheathed his dirk and placed his hands on either side of the Campbell clansman's head. Then, with a swift twist, he snapped his neck.

"They are almost here," Alastair proclaimed. "He wouldn't have risked this, even if he saw an opportunity for himself to try to kill me, if he didn't know that the rest of the men would soon be here."

"We must go back to Fortingall," I said, understanding.

"Yes." He nodded swiftly. "Donald and I will ride back to the keep alone to gather the men. Ian and Liam will take you back to town. Donald, once we arrive at the keep, it is your job to defend it. I will take my group of men out to meet the Campbells before they can get too near us."

I stepped forward and Alastair reached out to me, pulling me tightly to his side, but he didn't take his eyes off his men as he gave them their orders. "We will likely meet one of our lookout riders on the way. With the Campbells so close, they will have been spotted. We've no way to know how many other villages and croftings have already been hit along the way. We have gained precious time here. Don't waste it."

Alastair looked up to the setting sun and then back at us, his eyes steely and determined. "Night is almost upon us. We have the advantage."

The others strode away to remount their horses and

Alastair turned to me, his long fingers digging into the flesh of my arm. I reached up and took hold of him just as tightly as we stared into each other's eyes.

"Do not be doing anything vera foolish, do ye hear me?" he said.

His gaze roamed over my face with such intensity it was if he were trying to commit every line to memory. I was suddenly very scared.

"I could say the same to you." I grasped at his shirt-sleeves and tugged him closer until our bodies were pressed up against each other with barely enough space for a breath of wind to pass between us.

"You stay alive, Alastair MacGregor. Do you understand me? You stay alive, and you find me once this is done!"

Suddenly the air was gone from my lungs as I was crushed to him. Clinging to him in desperation, I poured all of my love into our kiss, determined to will him into surviving. If God was watching us at that very moment, I wanted there to be no doubt in His mind that we would not tolerate being taken from each other. Not now.

We broke apart, panting slightly, short of breath. Fire burned in Alastair's bewitching green eyes that I knew was reflected in my own blue ones. He ran a hand through the soft waves of my hair before clenching it in his fist. "Be safe," he whispered before releasing me. "And know that I love you."

Without another word he turned from me and

climbed up onto his horse. With one final glance he nodded to me before wheeling his horse around and galloping down the road toward the castle.

I stood there in the dirt road as the dust from the horse's hooves swirled around me, praying with all my might that this was not going to be the last time I saw the man I loved.

CHAPTER 32

*W*e rode back to Fortingall as fast as we could, our horses' hooves flying. We kicked up dust behind us as we raced against the setting sun.

The last rays of sunlight were just beginning to fade behind the horizon as we rode up to the first of the homes. Silently we spread out, but always kept within sight of one another as we alerted the people to the Campbells' imminent arrival. The air hummed with tension as we spoke in hushed voices, hurrying from house to house, ensuring that everyone would be prepared.

Weapons were drawn and windows were shuttered as people clung to their loved ones, waiting in tense silence to hear the first sounds of war.

Mrs. Fletcher, Sarah, Anna, Molly and I sat in silence as well. Others had come to defend the church with Ian and Liam, wanting to ensure that anyone needing to get inside for medical attention would be able to find their way through.

The maids sat shivering, despite the warmth. It was not a chill in the air that wracked their bodies, but the pervasive, lingering scent of fear. They clutched at each other's hands, heads bent in prayer. No matter the outcome of this night their lives, all of our lives, would be forever changed. Even if we defeated the Campbells, would others come? Would our secret be spread throughout the highlands for others to condemn? Would other clans decide to join the Campbells' cause and become determined to wipe us out?

These were the questions that ran through my head as I sat silently in a pew of the old church. I stared down at my hands clasped tightly in front of me and barely glanced up when Father MacGregor came and sat down beside me. We sat together like that, without saying a word, and waited, time passing by unchecked.

"They may not come tonight," said one of the girls behind me. Without turning around I could not tell which one.

Suddenly a wave of guilt crashed over me. It was possible that one or all of these young women could die tonight and yet I did not know them well enough to be able to tell them apart by voice alone.

My hands shook as I tried to bury the guilt. I tried to convince myself that it was unrealistic of me to want to know every single man, woman and child of clan

MacGregor, let alone know them intimately. But the guilt would not abate.

I spun around in my seat and stared at the three girls, trying to memorize every detail about them. Sarah with her blonde hair and sweet laugh. Anna with eyes like bluebells and a tongue so sharp it often got her in trouble with Mrs. Fletcher, earning her a quick swat with a spoon. And Molly. Molly was quiet, but always had a spark of intelligence and determination in her grey eyes.

Mrs. Fletcher sat slightly apart from the girls. She had been watching them closely but looked at me then. I felt as though she could read my mind and knew exactly what I was thinking. But I did not feel shame. Instead I felt an awareness and kinship. It was then that I understood that she had been doing the same thing. Even though Mrs. Fletcher had worked with these girls in the kitchen for years, she also felt a need to watch them, study them, and commit them to memory.

Sometimes, no matter how well you knew someone, it just wasn't enough, not nearly enough.

I thought back to the way Alastair had examined my face before leaving me just a few hours before.

No, it didn't matter. You would always feel as though you should have listened more, loved harder, paid closer attention. You would always regret that you hadn't cherished each moment, that you'd done little more than simply breathe the same air as the people around you.

I looked back over my life, reflecting fondly upon my father and my brother Fin. And as I sat there, trying to examine the tapestry of my life for any signs of black threads of regret, I breathed a sigh of relief when I discovered that I had none. No matter what hardships I had faced up until now, there was not a single moment I would have chosen to do differently.

My back straightened as a great weight lifted off of my shoulders. I was not yet ready to die, but if there was some other plan for me in the coming days I knew with all certainty that I could face my death without regret. And somehow, knowing that filled me with a great peace.

"We canna know for certain that they will come tonight," said Sarah. Her eyes shone with a tentative hope.

"You're right, Sarah," I told her with a sad smile. "None of us know for sure. They may not come tonight after all."

Sarah closed her eyes and let her shoulders sag with relief. I did not want to take her hope for the chance of one more peaceful night away. She was right; there was no guarantee. We did not know for sure that the attack would come tonight.

But I could feel it. I knew with absolutely certainty that the night had come. And while I didn't know what had happened to our riders, I trusted my instincts.

We should have had warning from our own men, but there was a very good chance that our scouts were being held captive even at that very moment and had no way to send word.

Whatever the reason, it no longer mattered. I could smell it on the wind and taste it on my tongue. The truth of it hung in the very air.

I stood and walked to one of the church's windows to look out into the night. A clansman walked past the window, not bothering to look inside, and instead continued to scan the area around him, tense and at the ready. I looked past him as far as I could deep into the black night. The muscles in my body were tight, like a coiled spring ready to snap.

It almost came as a relief when a few moments later the first screams tore through the air.

"I need more light over here!" I yelled to no one in particular without raising my head. We were all busy, but a moment later another lit candle was shoved toward me, helping to illuminate the wound I was attempting to dress.

The young man's forehead was covered in sweat, and droplets were dripping off of his ear onto the damp, makeshift bed beneath him. I longed to blot the moisture from his brow, to make him more comfortable in some way, but the slice across his chest was more important than the rivers of sweat that were running into his eyes.

My hands trembled lightly as I drew the thread through his overly warm flesh, trying to stitch the wound closed as carefully as possible.

I had never cared much for needlework when I was younger, and my tutor had considered me adequate at best. There was no denying that I had been far more adept at sitting a horse than I had been at needlepoint.

I focused intently, determined to stitch the wounded man back together to the best of my ability. I had never been so grateful for my father insisting that I continue with my lessons.

When I was finished I stepped back and gave his hand a reassuring squeeze. "You're all done now. Take some time to rest. I'll be back to check on you when I can."

He nodded weakly while I pressed a cloth to his face, finally able to dab him dry. Then I turned to the next man in need and settled in to see what I could do to ease his pain.

We worked steadily through the night, trying hard to ignore the clanging sounds of fighting outside. I wanted to go to the window, to look outside and see how we were faring. But whenever I thought I had a spare moment, the doors to the church would burst open and another poor soul would be brought inside in urgent need of our care. The world outside felt like a dream. Something real and yet not quite real, as though if I were to reach out and touch it my fingers would slip right through it without connecting.

Suddenly, I could smell the faint scent of smoke and out of the corner of my eye I could see a faint red glow outside. "Oh my God!" I ran to the window and looked outside.

I cried out at the sight, my hands flying to my mouth in horror. The buildings outside were ablaze. The Campbells had set the village on fire. It wasn't enough for them to kill us all; they wanted to erase any sign of us from the earth, to destroy the very memory of us.

Rage tore through me as I watched the scene outside. Men, women and wolves were fighting side by side, pushing the swarming group of Campbell men back from the church.

I looked around the church, at the women running back and forth administering what aid they could as Father MacGregor walked slowly up and down the rows of the dying, administering the last rites to those we had been unable to heal.

I looked down at the blood on my hands and then back out the window just in time to watch another of my clansmen fall to the ground, as a Campbell dressed all in black plaid ran him through with a sword.

I shook with fury and spun from the scene, marching toward the door of the church, tearing off my gown as I went. I stood before the doors clad only in my shift, then threw the doors open wide. I shrugged my shoulders and the shift fell to the floor. I heard gasps behind me as I stood naked in the church doorway, focused on the change.

"Lady MacGregor!" Mrs. Fletcher cried out. "You mustn't!"

I looked back over my shoulder at her, feeling the warmth from the fires of my burning town caressing my skin. I said nothing, but she understood. She would be unable to stop me.

I ran forward out of the church in a burst of speed, and felt the muscles and bones in my body shifting and realigning as I ran. I barely registered the looks of shock on people's faces as I ran naked past them before I lunged, completing my shift into wolf form.

I came down on top of a Campbell, knocking him down into the street, ignoring his screams as he threw his hands up to protect his face before I killed him.

I threw back my head and howled into the night, rallying the other wolves around me. Together we regrouped and began forcing the Campbells back, working in tandem to surround and decimate them in groups of three or four at a time.

The Campbells were one of the largest clans in the highlands, and Robert Campbell had enlisted more men to Allina's cause than we could have imagined. There was no telling the amount of damage they had done to the other towns. It they had used this kind of force to sweep across the rest of the lands, the farms and croftings were surely decimated.

Fueled by sorrow and rage, I threw myself into the

fray, killing blindly and letting my animal nature over-take me. Buoyed by the sight of me in my giant wolf form, my pure white coat almost glowing in the moon-light and streaked through with Campbell blood, the MacGregors gathered their strength and pressed on. Soon we had the last of the Campbells on the run and we split up to hunt them down before they could escape.

I turned the corner between two houses and found myself surrounded by a group of Campbells.

I lowered my head and growled, trying to back away slowly. They pressed forward with their swords drawn as I looked for an opening to attack. I had to be careful, not just of the sharpness of their blades but of being touched by them at all. They had come well prepared to destroy us thanks to Allina's treachery. All of their weapons had been coated in pure silver. Even a touch from the flat of their blades would burn.

I turned and ran, drawing them from the alley to more open space where I would not be so easily trapped. I moved quickly to take out the first man while the others encircled me. I howled in pain as my flesh burned when one of their blades sliced through my shoulder. Turning, I lunged at my attacker, throwing him against the wall of the nearest building, where he crumpled to the ground and collapsed.

The Campbells surrounded me and pressed me back, trying to block me in against the building behind me. Suddenly a brown wolf came out of nowhere and tore through the men. They screamed and tried to scatter but we ran them down and finished them off together.

I turned to look at the brown wolf, gratitude flowing through me.

"*Lady MacGregor.*" Graham's voice floated through my head.

"*Graham. Thank you.*" I projected the thought into his head, communicating with him silently.

I had been wrong all along. Graham really was trustworthy. I felt a pang of guilt about how hard I had been on him, but it had felt necessary at the time. When I looked at him I could see that he would not hold it against me in the future.

"*We have gathered all of the survivors that we could. We have to leave this place. More Campbells are already on their way.*"

"*There can't possible be more!*"

"*Word has arrived that Allina has married Robert Campbell. There will always be more.*"

I cursed as I ran with him to where he and his men had gathered all of the survivors that they could find. I looked around and saw Donald and Gregory, Ian and Liam, but could not see Alastair anywhere.

I shifted back into human form and my shift and gown were quickly pressed into my hands. The clansmen averted their eyes to give me some privacy while I clothed myself. While nudity was fairly common among those who could shift, it did not change the fact that I was the wife of the clan chief.

"Where is Alastair?" I asked the men as I dressed. "Where is my husband?"

"We've not seen him in some time, Glenna," said Donald. The worry was clear on his face. "We lost sight of him some time after the fighting broke out."

"You mean he's out there alone? We have to find him!" I demanded.

"There is no time," said Donald, shaking his head. "We have to get these people to safety and we have to do it now. Alastair will be all right, lass. I promise ye he'll find us."

But I knew that Donald could promise me no such thing.

We led our people away from the town and up into the mountains as Fortingall burned at our backs. I couldn't believe that we were being run from our homes. Not even the keep was safe. If Robert Campbell decided to alert the rest of the highland chiefs to our secret, the clans combined could easily surround our castle and tear it down brick by brick to get to us. We had no choice but to disappear.

We pressed on for hours up into the hills, with the bright glow of Fortinall behind us. When we felt that we had traveled far enough away to risk stopping to rest, I stood at the edge of the cliff and looked out across the long stretch of glen and forest below.

I focused on the bright ball of orange in the

distance as the first streaks of daylight began to caress the sky.

My heart ached as I gently placed a hand low on my stomach. I had felt the truth of it in my shift, which would be my last for the next nine months. Now my body would be incapable of taking wolf form—nature's way of protecting the life that was growing inside me.

CHAPTER 33

"My lady, my lady, come quickly!" Mrs. Fletcher cried as she shoved her head into my tent.

I wrapped my shawl tightly around my shoulders and hurried outside after her. Winter had come early that high in the mountains and I could already see my breath on the air. I moved carefully, with one hand on my belly. I was four months pregnant but some days I felt further along than that. The size of my stomach made me think that my child would easily grow to be as large as his or her father.

At the thought of Alastair I doubled over in pain. My heart felt as though it was being squeezed inside my chest and tears burned at my eyes. Four months. Four long months of searching and praying and there had been no sign of him.

I walked through the camp, vaguely aware of the

murmurs as I went, curious as to what had Mrs. Fletcher so excited. Then I froze in my spot, my body jerking as I stopped. I shook my head, unable to comprehend what my eyes were seeing.

Alastair strode forward through the camp with Graham at his side. Graham, who had been gone for days, weeks at a time, looking for him. Never giving up. After everything, Graham had been the one to bring him back to us.

I let out a sob and started running. Alerted by the sound, Alastair turned to me and let out a whoop as he ran to me. He grabbed me and swept me up into his arms, covering my face in kisses. His wild, unkempt beard scratched against my face.

"You're here!" I gasped as I tried to kiss every inch of his face while he kissed mine. "You're here, you're here! He found you." I burst into joyful tears and clung to him, shaking. The dam of sorrow that I had tried to keep under control broke and I sobbed into his neck as he held me.

"Not even God in heaven could keep us apart, my love. Is that not what I promised ye?" he whispered into my hair, his voice tight with emotion.

I nodded, laughing as I wiped away my tears. "Yes, yes, it is. You're a man of your word, Alastair MacGregor. And for that I've a gift for you."

I pulled back from him and placed his hand on the swell of my belly.

He looked down at my stomach and then up at my

face in wonder. He opened his mouth to speak but closed it when nothing came out. Shaking his head in disbelief, he looked down at my stomach again, where his child was growing inside.

"Glenna. Glenna, you're pregnant?"

"Yes," I laughed, my shock at seeing him changing into pure joy.

"You're going to have my child?" he asked again, as if unable to believe it.

"Yes!" I told him, laughing louder.

"You're going to have my child!" he shouted.

He lifted me off the ground again and I let out a happy shriek. I threw my arms around him and kissed him deeply as our people cheered.

Over the months we had found hundreds of MacGregors and had brought them here to safety. We knew there were more out there, and with my husband safely home we would continue to look for them. We would survive and we would rebuild.

We would have our children, and in time they would grow. Together, we would regain what had been stolen from us. But for now we would bide our time, regather our strength and allow ourselves to fade into legend until the time was right. Gone, but never forgotten. Eventually, we would take back what was ours. But for now, we would become the wolves of the mist.

The End

Thank you for reading Loved by the Highland Wolf. If you loved this story and can't wait to get your hands on more make sure you never miss a new release by signing up for my newsletter with the link below.

Stephanie Marks Newsletter